BOUNCE BACK.

BETTER.

STRONGER.

To those who are compelled to confront their deepest fears and find the strength to keep moving forward, no matter the obstacles life throws their way.

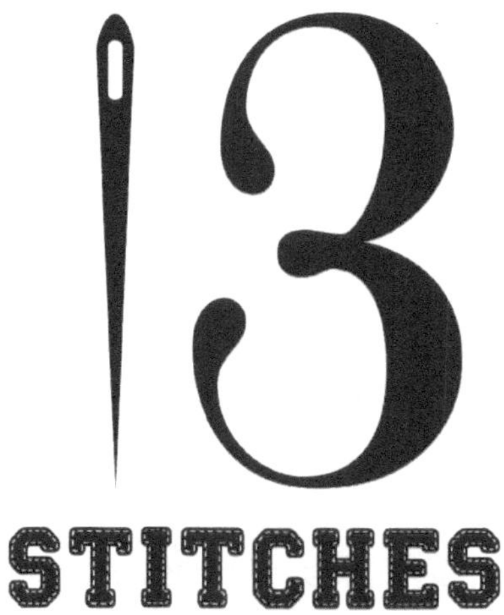

U-n-s-e-e-n

SARAB KAUR
SNEHA SINGH

ISBN
Paperback 979-8-89610-396-7
Hardcase 979-8-89724-989-3

Contents

FIRST STITCH

The Bubble Wrap

By Sneha Singh

From the other side of the phone, Samyukta said, *"Enough, Saahas! How many more times will you do this?"* Saahas, without responding much, said, *"Keep quiet, Yukta! I just NEED to do this!"* and gasping for breath asked the cab driver to halt.

Staring at her from the rearview mirror, the cabbie seemed to think to himself, *"I barely even started, lady, and weren't you the one in such a great hurry?"*

"Saahas, look at you, you're a young lady, living in one such quaint lane of this Mumbai Mahanagari. Look at all this lush greenery and these charming villas around you and then look at yourself, so vaguely imaginative and unnecessarily adventurous as a soul?" she questioned herself, *"Why are you always so eager to explore the world around you and that too, so critically?"* she continued thinking to herself as she was still on the call with Samyukta. *"You know, Yukta, today my heart is literally pounding with anxiety as I've this negative yet powerful urge to hasten back home, as if I'm late for home. I mean it could sound funny, but the moment I just stepped into the cab, claiming I was in a hurry to reach the office, I have this really important presentation in the town hall meeting that we have all been preparing for, for at least a fortnight now, I immediately had this urgency to reach back! Uff! Uff! Uff! My gosh! Like what kind of crap brain is this? All the possible negative thoughts, right at the moment when it's just not even needed,"* Saahas gasped.

"Nonetheless, the cabbie had to brake hard and came to a stop. I almost jumped out of the car and ran towards the entrance of the colony, rushing, heaving. And as I rounded the corner and caught sight of the house, my unease had grown stronger." she continued.

Doubt gnawed at her mind, and she couldn't shake away the feeling that something was amiss. Had she locked the front door? Had she closed all the windows? The thought of leaving her home vulnerable filled her with worry.

She picked up her pace, her footsteps echoing on the quiet street. The gentle breeze that usually brought her comfort now only heightened her sense of urgency. A million thoughts raced through her mind as she tried to recall if she had taken all the necessary precautions before leaving. Approaching the white picket fence that bordered her house, Saahas' heart sank. The sight of the unlocked gate intensified her fears. A chill ran down her spine as she quickly closed the gate, hoping that was the only thing she had forgotten. She rushed up the cobblestone path to the front door, her hands trembling as she fumbled for her keys. With a shaky breath, Saahas inserted the key into the lock and turned it slowly. To her relief, the door creaked open, revealing the familiar warmth and cosiness of her home. She stepped inside, only to find herself gripped by fresh doubts. Had she closed all the doors, windows, turned off the necessary gadgets, etc? *"The sound of my own heartbeat is deafening to my ears. Phew! This is such a bad feeling, ooh gosh what have I done?"* she kept murmuring to herself.

Determined to put her mind at ease, Saahas hurried through the house, checking each window one by one. As she went from room to room, she said to herself, *"Whoa, I love my house, I just really wish nothing ever happens to it,"* she again continued to mumble to herself. *"Each corner holds memories of laughter, joy, and the love of my family. The thought of anything happening to it constantly keeps making me even more anxious."*

Samyukta from the other side said, *"Is everything alright with the house?"* in a tone that was certain, everything was perfect. This was not the first time Samyukta was on the receiving end of such a conversation. It was for the *nth* time that she had heard Saahas speak these sorts of words. Contexts changed but the crux always remained the same.

Saahas sighed and said, *"Yukta, it was locked! The doors are all closed, balcony doors secured, windows bolted, mmm, the gas inlet is sealed as well, diya (lamp) is also put off, all electric fittings and electronics are the way they are supposed to be, shut. There's no house key I have left in any secret place for Meera Aunty to come and clean. She has one of her own. Phew. Geyser is also not left on. All my work is on my laptop and yes, I have my charger, right here in my bag. I am wearing the right formals – face... hair... my watch... check, check, check. OKAY! all good, yeah?!"*

Saahas is still on a call and almost talking to herself, without conscious thought.

Finally, after confirming that all of it was securely shut, Saahas felt a sense of relief wash over her. *"Wait, but it's not over as yet,"* she continued to talk to herself with Samyukta still over the call, listening to all the hyper conversations Saahas is having with herself. As she made her way to the back door, she noticed a glimmer of sunlight reflecting off the doorknob. Panic surged within her, and she froze in her pants.. The door was slightly ajar.

Saahas' mind raced, trying to remember if she had closed it properly before leaving. With a deep breath, she mustered her courage and slowly pushed the door open. To her immense relief, the latch had caught just enough to prevent it from swinging open entirely. She quickly secured the lock and leaned against the door, letting out a sigh of relief.

"Phew, everything is perfect! Ok, now I have got to lock the house again!" saying so, she locked the door and continued to talk to Samyukta, *"Scrutiny, once again! It's locked properly, right Yuktu?"* Samyukta sighs and says, *"Yes honey, it is! Now if you don't mind, please go and see if the poor cabbie is still there and if he is, THEN GET GOING."*

Samyukta continues, *"All the best for your presentation, Ahas. Don't keep revising it. I, for real, have got to go for now. I've to drop Sri off to school and head straight out for the office. Okay. Good day, hon. Love you!"* and the call disconnects.

These two addressed each other as Ahas and Yukta/Yuktu since they were bench mates in the third grade.

Saahas, feeling reassured, gets right back into the cab and tells the cabbie happily, *"Thank you for holding up! I had to recheck if I left the house the way I was supposed to. Not like I didn't check before leaving, but I had to recheck."*

Saying so, Saahas kept talking about some random stuff to the cabbie and to herself, rehearsing her presentation and then re-rehearsing it throughout her journey to the office.

With all the hustle and bustle and struggles of the day, little did she realise, it was time to head back home. As she walked out of the office, she started to reflect upon her day and thought to herself, *"Why did I even put so much pressure on myself thinking - I've not locked the door, I've not done this, what if my presentation didn't go well, what if I was not prepared enough?"*

This thought had struck her a couple of times every now and then. She realised that most of her actions were based around the idea of not being prepared enough for a possible problem, the consequent risk, and then, as a matter of fact, risk aversion, most importantly.

It was as if she was living in an emergency mode in her head. As if there was some imminent danger just around the corner she was sensing and saving herself from. As if she wanted to be prepared for everything unseen, unheard, unknown.

A couple of days passed, and Saahas continued to do her regular activities at work. Her household chores and running errands kept her busy.

Although the thought of why she was always burdening herself was something she wasn't able to dissect. The thought didn't leave her head while she did whatever else she was doing externally.

"Why the exigency? Why the strain? Why the urgency?" she kept cross-questioning herself. As a result, Saahas started noticing her own behaviour and reading more and more about it online. She started interacting with all the AIs she could about it.

One fine evening, Saahas was to stop by after a long week at work to see Samyukta. They both usually stayed loyal to the same specific place, where the entire staff was familiar with them to the extent they even knew what Saahas and Samyukta would prefer to order. They both usually, more often than not, preferred to take the corner-most table in the open-air section of *'Creme De La Coffee'*, so they could see the view of the entire city from there.

Saahas reached a bit later than the time they had decided they would. Samyukta has been used to Saahas showing up later than the said time, the reason being her second-guessing every tiny bit she perpetrates. This was an open secret by now. Samyukta even catechised Saahas on a couple of junctures.

"And there you are, Miss. Double, Triple. Quadruple checks… " Samyukta said and got up to hug Saahas. They both hugged enthusiastically and took their respective seats.

"Yukta," Saahas says, *"Why did you address me as Miss Double, Triple, Quadruple check, almost as if you were going to count to infinity?!"*

They both sheepishly smile at each other and then get on with talking about what they would want to eat, how the week has been, who did what, who wore what, what all happened at their workplaces, in their respective societies, etc.

And then, how Saahas got her nails done on the way to work in the middle of the week because she was so bored and wanted something new to obsess over, about Sri and how his class teacher doesn't interest him and about everything they had to catch up on. About all possible things that could be spoken regarding anything and everything, under the sun. They even cracked up thinking how crazy they are and how anyone listening to their conversation can find them so random.

Samyukta whines haphazardly, *"You know Ahas, Sri's class teacher during the PTA meeting said, 'Do you know Mrs. Dadra, your Sriansh Dadra is 5 years old, and he refuses to behave or even think of himself as a child. He rather chooses to behave more like an adult. He asks his fellow mates to address him as SD and not Sri or Sriansh. When I ask, 'How are you today, Sriansh?' he replies saying he's a cool dude!'"*

Saahas and Samyukta crack up in sprouts of laughter.

Arbitrarily Saahas called on Samyukta, *"Yuktu, tell me why did you say I am Miss Double, Triple, Quadruple check again? It almost seemed as if you would keep at it for eternity."*

They both had a hearty laugh while Saahas had not even concluded her statement.

Samyukta said, *"Oh Ahas, you know, you do not have to take it otherwise. Although, why, WHY do you keep rechecking, reconfirming so much? It's almost as if you don't trust yourself. Do you really not trust your own self, Ahas?"* she gasps.

Suddenly Saahas looked at the sky, meddling with her hair, settling her thickly kohl-lined eyes, and said, *"You know, that's some food for thought for me. I've been pondering why I keep doing this and while you come up with this query, I've just come to realise it actually takes a toll on me. This has been concerning me too. I have understood that this whole thing makes me feel like the world out there is full of dangers I must protect myself from. I am on this roll to save myself from something that might never even happen. You know it's like I am my teacher out to warn myself of anything that I may be doing wrong. There are days I am so anxious, I start hyperventilating at times because of not being able to recheck what I've done & until I do, I'm not at peace. It gives me serious fatigue on days and maybe some gastric issues as well; it could be psychosomatic, I am not even sure! I learnt all of that while reading about it online."*

"I think I developed this a lot more, quite seriously after I moved out of my parents' house and started living all by myself. Perhaps because until I was with them, I felt like they had me in control and took care to see I made no mistakes, not even the tiniest possible ones. They almost hovered over me, to take care and control of my health and safety and make each act impeccable."

Samyukta, quite shocked and surprised at the same time, says to Saahas, *"I have brought this up in the past with you, but it didn't bother you as much or should I say, not at all, what is up Ahas? You okay?"* and she holds Saahas' arm to express concern and warmth.

Saahas continued without even taking a deep breath, *"You know when I was in school, my mom made me revise, re-revise and then re-revise repetitively. She would randomly ask me questions from my portion while doing random activities like eating, getting dressed and until I was ready and off to school, even while we waited at the end of our lane for my school bus to arrive."*

"She would keep reinstating if I had heard the teacher correctly, if I was fine and didn't need to visit the washroom time and again. This was, of course, out of concern, but it was so repetitive that it stuck in my psyche that it's not okay to not second guess. So throughout school and college, I kept feeling uncomfortable on exam days when I had not re-revised. You know, it's not possible as your studies start to grow. So, you know, it became more than a habit. Consequently, even before

I realised, this became more than just a habit. It became a very major part of my personality!"

"And even now, an important day in the office will not pass without me getting all hyper and anxious starting days prior to the big day. It's like I was raised to stay protected from any possible mishap."

"When we went to buy a cycle for me, we also bought a helmet, knee and elbow pads and whatnot to protect me from falling. I mean, of course, I understand my parents wanted the best for me and were trying to protect and guard me, and they did so as well, but other kids didn't have all these and they fell, must have even hurt themselves, and then they were possibly never scared again."

"Although, you know, in my case, I was not only scared of being hurt but I also always had to protect myself. I've always and forever lived under the pressure of being careful, protecting myself from being hurt, from any unforeseen dangers. I've always lived under the pressure of having my shield up, my guards up and above, all the time. It was instilled in me, as a child, that I'd to avoid any possible danger."

"I was taught not to leave a lit candle in its enclosed stand when I leave the room, even if it was for a couple of minutes. Turning the gas off at the main switch was mandatory each time cooking was completed. Talking on the phone, even in the kitchen premises, let alone inside the kitchen, was banned because the cell phone battery could heat up from the burner's heat and explode. Like WHAT? Seriously? Do you understand?" Saahas said and sighed.

While Samyukta was still collating and contemplating what Saahas had just said.

Saahas effused, *"Gosh! I just realised while I spoke all this out loud to you, that I was raised by OVERPROTECTIVE PARENTS! AND that is precisely why I have grown to be this woman who is a risk averter, socially awkward. Just think about it! Oh God! I just never really pondered upon why I lived under so much duress. What brought about all the strain I was putting on my brain!"* panting, Saahas kept looking up at the clear, blue sky filled with white, snowy, scattered clouds!

What protective layers do you put around your emotions, and what might happen if you popped them?

SECOND STITCH

The Faith Paradox

By Sarab Kaur

"Hello there, mole No.1, mole No.2, and other cute yet ugly-looking moles! So the thing is I am biased towards the bigger moles on my face, you'd ask me why?" The crowd laughed out louder and screamed *"why."* As Guru, the comedian, walks onto the stage, he looks pretty relaxed. He is wearing jeans and a t-shirt, looking like they've been worn a lot. His hair is thinning, and he has lots of soft lumps on his face. He does not seem bothered by his appearance or the fact that he is single. He places the mic into the stand and continues, *"I'll tell you why, imagine these bigger moles are like my face prints, just like we have thumbprints. They make me who I am, I mean c'mon if someday I get them removed surgically, would you even recognise me? No, right? I mean, yeah, well, you could figure out me being me, but you know how back in olden times we had the birthmark option on our passports? Mine kept changing over the years because each year I had a new mole and that first old mole was now a bigger one!"* Guru laughed and mocked himself. The room echoed with the audience's laughter.

"Imagine my phone would never unlock if these moles disappeared overnight!" Then an audience member says out loud, *"The face recognition function on the phone wouldn't work on you!"*

"Absolutely right!! Guy with a head, whom I can't see. Because of the spotlight and whom I don't know, yeah, it won't open - it won't recognise my face," Guru agreed, while trying to dodge the spotlight to see who it was, yet continued *"The phone would say face unrecognised, then I'll have to make new ones with a marker man! Or I may have to get creative with some black clay!"* and the crowd

laughed as Guru made exaggerated hand movements and hilarious expressions with eyebrows and the occasional smirk.

"You have been a great audience. I am given 5 minutes on stage though moles consumed a bit more!! I'll see you soon with another whole mole story!" The crowd hooted and cheered for Guru, and he shouted back, *"Thank you, everyone, for coming and for your enthusiasm. I'll be back soon with more stories! That's my set, guys!"* He waved goodbye to the audience and made his way offstage.

Even though he made people laugh, Guru was lonely. He was almost forty and still single. While his friends were getting married and some of them already had families. He had a boring 9-5 job and after sunset, he'd head to comedy clubs. There, he would tell jokes that made people laugh, and he felt alive, felt seen, felt known. He frequently laughed at his funny body structure, the oddly shaped head that had scanty grey hair. His jokes mostly were about the weirdest moles on his face and wondered if God cursed him with it, as he ridiculed them. He used various voice modulations to describe the moles on his face that made the audience laugh even before he uttered a word. He was their favourite *'Mole Wala Act'* (the one with the mole act). And when he was not too busy, Guru enjoyed spending his time looking after his neighbour's pet while they were away.

However, today something unusual happened, something he was not expecting at all. It was not his fortunate day. Just before his time on stage, at his open mic venue, he got a phone call. As Guru saw the number flash on his screen, he thought to himself, *"Eh, there comes my favourite call. Just another volunteering opportunity at the Mehra's."* He was extremely curious to know how soon he could be there for Faith. And so he picks up the call with excitement, *"Hey! Mehra ji.. what time do I come over for Faith?"*

Faith is a super shy, quiet, and lovely 4-year-old golden retriever dog, well in this case a bitch. Whenever the Mehra's went for their quirky, impromptu getaways for a couple of days, Guru used to dog-sit Faith. *"Hello Guru, how are you? Hoping we didn't disturb you, do you have a minute to talk?"* said Mehra ji with anxiousness and semi-guilt.

"We're calling you at this odd hour of the day, to share some news. Since you have been so close to our family, Faith is as much of a pet to you as to us. We wanted to inform you that our family is moving away for good, and we'd been so busy packing that it just slipped off our mind to share this with you before today. We will leave within the next couple of hours." Guru listened to this piece of information, keenly with the background noise of the other stand-up comedians and the laughter of the crowd. Guru was trying to keep up with Mehra ji's words and as he processed the news he went into a bit of a shock, he immediately asked, *"Moving away? Suddenly? Hope everything is fine?"* wondering if he heard correctly.

"Oh yes, everything is fine. We've been meaning to move away for quite some time now. The trips we used to take around the country were to check out larger properties, where Faith can have a better garden space of her own. Also, I can sit and relax as I have recently retired. We Mehras will have a grand and brand-new beginning."

Guru was confused and somehow annoyed by the sudden news. Before Guru could say or ask anything, Mehra ji said, *"We will leave in about an hour's time. It'll be great if you can come over and meet us for one last cup of chai (tea) and meet Faith before she leaves. I am sure she would love seeing you and would love to say goodbye and it'll be a great opportunity for us to thank you in person for always being there to help dog-sit for Faith."*

The only thing that struck him was his best friend was being taken away. He gulped and nervously said, *"But I am in the middle of an open mic right now, and it will take me more than an hour to finish my turn, and by the time I reach you, it'll take another couple of hours. Is it possible for you to postpone leaving by an extra hour? I'll try to be there as soon as I finish my performance."*

"Uhh... I'll ask Mrs. Mehra if she has the time to extend; you know these wives, they want everything done in a timely fashion. I'll try to pull in the extra hour, but try to be here pronto because we have other meetings and places to be. It is a long road trip, and we have planned pit stops along the way. Ok, see you then." And he hangs up the phone.

As Guru processes this news, his heart becomes heavy. Often referring to her as his soulmate and his best friend, Faith was like his therapist. She would listen to his emotional stories and wallow in love, her eyes beaming with joy and pure emotions, wagging her tail, and licking him with kindness and empathy. Over these 4 years, Guru and Faith had become each other's best friends, or soulmates as Guru called it. Faith was like a ray of sunshine, always eager to play and showering Guru with affection. Every time he visited, Faith would bound towards him, her tail wagging furiously and her eyes shining with excitement. They'd spend hours together in the park, chasing after balls and frolicking in the grass. Guru could not stop himself from having flashbacks, couldn't control the panicky feeling while reminiscing the good old times and moments. There were times when they would simply sit together under the shade of a tree, enjoying the peaceful silence and the gentle breeze. But what he loved most was the way Faith would look at him with such adoration and trust. It warmed his heart to know that in Faith's eyes, he was her favourite human. When they walked back home together, Guru could not help but feel grateful for their simple yet deep bond. But now, his best friend is departing. As Guru was backstage staring into his phone looking at videos and photos of Faith and reminiscing their adventures! Right then, he is interrupted by his manager. *"Guru, it's Time! You're up in two minutes, and your sponsors are watching you. If you want the country tour, give it your best shot!"*

Inhaling deeply with a mind full of thoughts and flashbacks, he plasters a smile and walks into the cheering crowd as his set is being announced. Squinting his nose, looking at the sponsors, he sarcastically remarks with the mic in his hand *"What better way to mock myself onstage, amongst this huge, classy crowd, than to receive mockery in person, eh?"* The crowd cracks up and starts howling over his first line itself. Pointing his finger at a random person in the audience who laughed louder than the others, he says, *"Hey there, you the red hoodie guy, I won't leave you, my moles are going to monitor you like a CCTV, when they see even the slightest of a chance where you'd mock me, I will jump right in and do it myself!! Because they're my moles!! Not yours, you Mr. Moleless person!"* The crowd whistled, clapped, and laughed. He could see the sponsors smiling, looking around and witnessing him in his full glory. *"So you know just like all of you, I have friends of my own! And mind it when I say my own they literally live on me,"* nodding his head, looking up at the ceiling pretending God's right there watching over him, he asks, *"Why God! Why have you given me these moles!"* emphasising the 7 moles which were of different sizes. He pointed out the biggest one for the audience to see clearly and laughed along saying, *"This is my friend number 1. I have had him since my childhood. It has literally grown with me. And the funny thing is with pimples, one can coat it with a good concealer or foundation, but moles, no they are goddamn black pepper-sized spongy moles! They are big and are right up on my cheeks and nose screaming at the crowd, look at us, look at us, we are Guru's pot-moles, you know how they refer to Mumbai being a kingdom of potholes, just like that, I have my pot-moles!"*

And the crowd went crazy with laughter. They hooted and clapped thunderously. Right then, he got lost for a few seconds. Those few seconds were the longest. He suddenly had a flashback of the phone call he received earlier. Guru froze and went blank. Suddenly, there were tears in his eyes, and he lost the vibe. The sponsors and the audience all felt guilty for laughing out loud over the mole joke.

The crowd went *"Aww"* confused about what just happened. The event manager stared at Guru in horror, wondering why he was doing this. Out of all the days, why today? He has never done this before. Hey, it is a stand-up comedy open mic after all. Guru could not hold it together; he broke down, went down on his knees, and cried for half a minute on stage. In the room full of laughter, there was an awkward silence. He gathered some courage, picked up a bottle of water, gulped in heavy sips, and continued with something new. Something that was unexpected from a comedian.

Glancing at the crowd, he smiled with tears in his eyes. *"So now you guys have one more reason to mock me, 'Oh look, Guru is weeping on a comedy open mic.' I'll love to fill you in, and I know it's of no interest to you but since I am on stage and these are my few minutes, I am going to do what I want to."* He shrugged his shoulders, and the crowd responded with confused giggles. Guru looked at the sponsors with fear of being denied on the country tour for stand-ups, yet he went on with his story, *"So, earlier just before getting on the stage, I received a call from my neighbour, telling me they were moving away. Now you would wonder, why would a middle-aged guy cry if the neighbours are moving away. Right? So the thing is, I am in love."*

"Aaaah!" exclaimed the crowd. A few screamed *"Oooh mole has a love story,"* and Guru immediately responded to them, *"Oh, ya that's a nice one for my next stand-up, if only the sponsors and managers allow me after this weeping session!!"* The crowd and sponsors laughed it off, and a few cheered for him and appreciated his efforts, which gave him more strength.

And he continued, *"So like I said, I am in love, not with my neighbour, but with their pet, and her name is Faith. She is this beautiful golden retriever whom I used to take care of while these neighbours of mine were touring out of town. I gladly volunteered to be there for her. Faith and I have become best friends in the past 4 years. I've known her ever since she was a puppy, and the sad part is she is being taken away. I don't know if I should even say this because technically she isn't even mine. Just a neighbour willing to pet-sit their dog – 'if you know what I mean?' babysit... pet-sit? And right now, my biggest concern is not the sponsors. Sorry, yeah, it's just something too touchy for me today. I don't know if I will make it to bid farewell to the family and Faith because they leave in an hour's time, and I am here, an hour away doing what I do best: cracking a joke. But look at the irony, today I cannot do that as well."*

"Today I feel like I truly am a joke. I always thought Faith was mine. But look, God has just responded in the most awful way ever." God probably says, 'Your moles are your best friends, they themselves are your pets and your soulmates, not Faith, eh?'" He felt rejected, smirked and looked down at the floor.

Guru never felt this heavy-hearted in all these years. Not even when he was bullied at school for having a funny skeletal body structure or scanty hair. His heart sank, and it was going away with Faith. Guru's 8 minutes on the open mic were up.

After Guru's stand-up act, the event manager pulled him aside. *"Guru, we need to talk,"* the manager said, looking serious.

"What's up?" Guru asked, feeling nervous.

The manager sighed. *"Look, your talent is considerable, but you went off-script. You spent too much time talking about your dog and getting emotional. This is a comedy show, not a therapy session."*

Guru's heart sank. *"I know, I just got carried away. My dog means a lot to me."*

The manager shook his head. *"I get it, but you need to think about the audience. We had potential sponsors in the crowd tonight, and you might have missed out on future opportunities because of that emotional tangent."*

Guru felt guilty. *"I'm sorry, I didn't realise."*

The manager sighed again. *"Just be more mindful next time, okay? We want to keep this show successful."*

Guru nodded. *"Got it. Thanks for letting me know."*

As they parted ways, Guru could not shake the feeling of disappointment in himself. He knew he needed to find a balance between sharing his personal stories and keeping the audience entertained. But he also knew what he was losing. He was losing a loyal friend who never judged him or laughed at him. That dog brought him peace. Instead of saying goodbye to his favourite dog in the world, he let it be the way it was.

Later that night, Guru took a walk in the park, where Faith loved to be. As he sat in her favourite spot, surrounded by trees and quiet, he could see that Mehra's car wasn't there anymore, their house lights were off, and everything was quiet. Extremely quiet. It felt like Faith had taken away his laughter, his love for pets, and worst of all, his sense of humour.

It appeared Guru cracked under the pressure, never to crack a joke again.

How do your beliefs shape your reality,
and what challenges them?

THIRD STITCH

The Invisible Threads

By Sneha Singh

Amrita, while climbing the stairs towards her bedroom on the third floor, looked at the lane through the staircase; it looked dark and gloomy, with a wretched vibe of despondency. She thought to herself, *"I was an epitome of grace and charm, but behind my lost radiant smile, today there is so much. The hidden weariness that comes from the household chores I toil over each day. My beaming, cheerful smile has withered away from all the verbal defaming that has been falling into my ears."* She sighed as she felt tired to climb those few stairs.

In this small town of Ludhiana, Punjab, newly-wed Amrita, who had been known to have a magnetic personality that drew people to her, with an aura that radiated opinionated energy, had just a few days ago tied the knot with her now-beloved husband, Rajiv. It was peak winter season; the days had grown shorter, and the nights had turned colder. The warm festivities of the wedding were all over, and Amrita found herself immersed in the responsibilities of her new home.

As the chores around dinner ended, on that chilly winter evening, Amrita entered her bedroom after a hard day of toil, seeking respite from the cold. Her delicate fingers trembled as she switched on the warm spotlights, filling the room with a quiet, comforting glow.

Her bedroom was beautifully adorned with traditional Mexican paintings. She then reflected on the culture of the place her husband resided in at present and the place she thought was going to be her cherished home-to-be. Far away from her thoughts in Mexico City, she was here in her bedroom, in Ludhiana. This bedroom now felt like a sanctuary, away from the outside world, to her, like a place where she could be herself without any pretences.

Feeling the icy sting on her skin, Amrita decided to turn on the heater to create a cosy haven. As the room slowly warmed, she felt her tense muscles begin to relax. She let out a deep sigh, feeling the exhaustion from a long day's work gradually dissipate. The warmth enveloped her, and she felt a sense of relief, a reminder that despite all her responsibilities, all the emotional turmoil, she deserved this moment of tranquillity.

Amrita sat on the edge of her bed, thinking to herself, *"I cannot help but reminisce about all the details of the day I first arrived in this new home of mine. The treatment I received was such a cultural shock for me. At this very moment, it is barely around thirty days ago, yet it feels like years have passed by, putting up with all that is weighing me down. The initial excitement, nervousness, and anticipation of what the future held for me and Rajiv have all vanished into thin air. I miss my carefree days with my parents, the late-night giggles with my family, my friends, and the familiar surroundings of my childhood home."*

She thought about her new family, *"My in-laws, shouldn't they have welcomed her with open arms? Isn't that how a new bride is welcomed? They told my parents they would treat me like their own daughter, and it all seems so very far away from reality at this very moment. Everything that was communicated now seems like fiction."* She still yearned for the familiarity of her childhood home. Her thoughts turned to her husband, *"Rajiv is back to what he calls home, his comfort zone, there in Mexico City, in just eighteen days of being married. I miss the gentleness in his words from our dating days, his loving gaze during the umpteen ceremonies of our big fat Indian wedding, and the way he made me laugh during the days of our courtship. I miss the sound of my laughter."*

Amrita had known herself to be the woman who exudes confidence and power in every step. *"I have always navigated life with my fearless attitude, being the vehemently assertive woman with unwavering conviction. People who knew me had known Amrita for her outgoing nature and boundless energy."* Amrita spoke loudly to herself.

"Nonetheless, now I am struggling to help myself find that woman in me." She continued to speak aloud to herself.

Amrita brought this up with Rajiv over a couple of video calls that they had exchanged in the last few days, while she was here in her unfamiliar, non-welcoming space with her in-laws.

She tried to remind him, *"Rajiv, do you remember the way we used to laugh together? The difference between our courtship days and now is that I was happier then and you, you... were someone who felt familiar back then, and that was just a couple of days ago. How has so much changed in such little time?! I want to be happy again, Rajiv. I want to laugh again with you."*

However, all her words were in vain. Rajiv couldn't seem to be any less bothered about whatever she would say. He only now knew that his parents weren't happy with her. In retaliation, he made her feel bad and incompetent about being the sort of daughter-in-law she came along to be. He remarked, *"My parents have been putting up with your shortcomings."*

She failed to understand or even make any sense of what was being portrayed versus what the reality in fact is.

"I feel insane. I am seriously starting to doubt myself." "Is there something truly wrong with me, for real? What am I doing so incongruously?" Amrita is now just going on talking to the wall in the line of her vision, sitting under the warm, mild spotlights, with the heater on, also looking at the vibrant wallpaper on the wall diagonally opposite to where she was sitting, as if the walls were real people listening to and empathising with her. These walls alone were her companions now. She would talk to them time and again.

"I am not disrespecting my in-laws. I'm doing all the work I'm expected to do. Although no matter what all I do, no one seems to be content about any of it. I have single-handedly taken on all the household duties in my stride. Is that all? Is that what I was married into this family for?"

Amrita indignantly continued to speak aloud to the walls, *"Is marriage merely associated with handling domestic responsibilities for a woman? Why is the weight of these regressive gender roles only for the woman to carry? And do so with a smile while you ignore the contempt?!"*

At this very moment, the cold winter breeze brushed against the windowpane, making her shiver. But Amrita was not just cold from the weather - she felt a hint of loneliness creeping into her heart. She realised that amidst the excitement of the wedding and the busy household routines, she had hardly spent any time alone to reflect on her feelings.

As she sat there, a tear gently rolled down her cheek, catching her by surprise.

Amrita introspected as she spoke to the walls, *"My opinions have been silenced, my education, the achievements I have made through my work have been rendered worthless, my lively conversations have been muted to whispers."*

She wiped away the tears that were now blurring her vision, not wanting to succumb to sadness.

She picked up her phone to call Rajiv, but, recalling her last conversation with him, she felt it was better to keep her peace rather than listening to him accuse her of things she had not done, listening to him tell her the negative interpretations of her interactions with his parents. Instead, she chose to swipe through the photos on her phone.

Amrita scrolled through some positive quotes on her phone and tried to feel rejuvenated. Consequently, she ended up coming across pictures of herself, her family, the way they all waltzed together one evening. She started to reflect upon how poised they were, how highly educated, loved, and respected they were as a family.

She saw pictures of herself at the annual employees' meeting where she represented her department to show all they had accomplished as a team and how they could implement new strategies for better global reach. Pictures that reflected her stature among her colleagues and friends.

She realised that none of it was able to help her feel like it was all okay, like it was acceptable to feel emotionally and mentally tired, like sometimes not even seeking support from loved ones could make all the difference.

The winter night felt harsh, as all other nights. Amrita could not envisage a bright future, filled with hope or promises of a better tomorrow.

With her ankles feeling sore and a persistently achy back, Amrita lay flat on the bed, alone in the room and told herself, *"So, you're officially Mrs. Someone, Mrs. Rajiv Bhardwaj to be precise, for almost thirty-eight days now. And mind you, you are not yourself? Miss Amrita Kaul? Not that highly educated, city girl, working for an MNC and making her mark in FinTech anymore, is it?"* she groaned, *"I have lost touch with my own identity! Was I that unapologetically empowered woman, really? Was I that bubbly, full of life woman, ready to face every challenge of life? Oh, is that so? Well, I guess so, for what I'm being told!"* saying, so she opens the camera of her phone and looks at herself.

Amrita and Rajiv were in their mid-30s and hence were pretty well-established in their respective careers.

Her mother-in-law's words echoed in her ears, *"You are a nobody. Just nobody, except a daughter-in-law, a wife, and a daughter. You have no other identity. Your duty is to take care of your in-laws and husband, that is all! Why are you sad and crying all the while? You are getting your meals and clothes right; you should be happy with such a complete life!"*

Amrita looked at herself in the selfie camera as she lay flat on the bed and pondered, *"You don't look like you. Your eyes have no spark, lacklustre face. Huh! These mandatory newlywed ornaments, the vermillion smeared in your hair, these noisy bangles and look at your cracked, flaky fingertips caused due to household chores done single-handedly, with no help, as if you were a hired cook and a house help, exposed to such unpleasantries in this harsh winter? They don't look good on you!"* her relentless thoughts getting intense, *"Not like I have an issue with the household chores, we all do it. This is my home and I want to do everything to make it a happy, hygienic space for all of us. Nevertheless, why me alone? Why can't I be offered a bit of help at the very least? Why can't I be spoken to in a tone that is not demeaning? Why can't the surrounding humans be a little human towards me?"*

Amrita shuts the phone and closes her eyes, hoping to fall asleep. Her eyes feel exhausted, yet with her closed eyes, she starts to see the scenes of how she and Rajiv got married, how they looked so cute, like they were completely into each other, kind of a couple. She smiles, remembering moments from their pre-wedding photoshoot where she was wrapped in his arms, posing for a picture-perfect moment. She said to him, *"You know, Rajiv, I am so in love with you and I absolutely adore your romantic streak. Mr. Husband-to-be, don't you dare get any less romantic even at the time of marrying our children off!"* to which he smiled, and they kissed, cracked into laughter and Voila! So many candid pictures were captured in that moment!

However, now all of which has possibly changed and what was really behind the scenes? It kept playing in Amrita's mind how he made her feel completely horrible about herself, how he portrayed the wrong image of her in the eyes of his family, how he misinterpreted events and manipulated the situation into making it all appear as if he was the victim, how this family that should be welcoming her to be one among them is completely non-accommodating of her, how she is being made to feel insignificant and inconspicuous. In a trice, she opens her eyes and looks up at the white ceiling. With shock in her eyes, she affirms to the white ceiling, *"I'm being ill-treated!"*

"And for what? For being a new bride? For being a woman?"

"Are these the sort of heinous people we read about? Did this actually happen in real life to a real woman? And that woman being me? What should I do with this feeling of humiliation that I am not able to withstand? Go back home, forever? What will people think of my parents? Am I tolerating all of this due to societal duress?"

There's horror in her thoughts. She tells herself, *"Calm down, baby girl. Maybe it's just the jitters of being in a completely new environment. You chose to marry cross-culturally; it will have repercussions. And either way, anything new has its fair share of discomfort. You will be just fine."*

As Amrita reassured herself, she tried to close her eyes and overlook the yellow light falling straight into them. She left the light on because in the past twenty-two days of being in this room, she was managing to sleep alone through the night after Rajiv left for Mexico City. The room she and her newly wedded husband, Rajiv, shared for eighteen days until he flew back to Mexico. He chose to enter the room each day after she was fast asleep for all the eighteen days he happened to be with her.

Amrita wondered and questioned Rajiv's parents, *"Why does Rajiv never come home before 12 am?"* She could never understand why a newly married man, who has only a few days with his wife before he flew back to his workplace in Mexico City, would never come home until she's asleep. Why would he never be interested in having a conversation with his wife?

The night was cold, and in all the layers of clothes Amrita was wearing, she still felt frozen. She could neither dissect her emotions nor believe what she was sensing. All of this left Amrita lifeless and hysterical. She had no idea how to deal with so much all at once. With this hustle in her head, she happened to doze off.

A couple of hours into the harsh wintery night, she found herself awake holding the phone in her hands, staring at the screen. It might have been about 3 am or so. The much-awaited call from her newly wedded husband, Rajiv, was flashing on the phone. The contact picture of him, with a big smile, flashed on her screen along with his name. She told him, still staring at his picture, without answering the call, *"It's messy right now, sweetie, but you know, seeing your name makes me smile, makes me want to still feel buoyant. Perhaps we didn't get our due share of time together,"* and then she answered the call.

This was always *'their'* time. After the whole day of showing up and living their individual lives, they always managed to catch up with each other, wish each other a good night, and go off to sleep.

One and a half years of long-distance dating before they tied the knot, and now soon after their marriage, they had again gone back to being in courtship.

She answered the call, still sounding husky, and in deep slumber, *"Hello, baby,"*

They spoke for a while, and then she said to him, *"Technically, we are still dating and in a long-distance relationship, although now as a newly married couple. You know, dating after marriage is very different for me compared to 'dating' before marriage."*

Little did she realise that now the motive of these calls had changed. He now just needed the smallest statement from her to steer the entire conversation in the direction that would throw her off the cliff. He said, *"Why would you say that? What's the difference from then and now?"*

Amrita said, *"That's very insensitive of you to say, Rajiv! You're asking me what is the difference? I can't tell you the difference because this is a whole new life, like a reincarnation within the same life, for me. At least in a reincarnation you do not have to unlearn and relearn, you just start afresh and in this case, considering we are grown adults it's beyond difficult to adapt to a whole new level of expectations pouring in 360°!"* she continued, *"Nothing really changed for you, no? You don't have new people, new surroundings, a culturally new family and new city to deal with, neither did you have to switch from being in working professional mode to housewife mode, at least a normal housewife gets treated as a woman of the house, gets to see her husband every day..."*

To which Rajiv interrupted, *"So you mean living with my family is such a herculean task? Do you even know how my old parents are living and putting up with you? And your unmatched standards, that you seem to be 'showing off' to them! My aged parents are being so nice to you and this is how you talk about them?"*

Amrita is in utter shock now. Not sure if she should be sad, hurt, or upset about what she just heard him say in a tone that completely left her shattered. Also, because she knows in her heart that she's being emotionally bruised and here she is getting to hear quite the opposite of reality. In her head, she suddenly transports to the scene where she is being asked to wash the sheets and linens she uses by herself and not along with everyone else's because she was almost untouchable in the views of her in-laws, which conveniently changed when cooking and cleaning chores came onto the picture.

Amrita's mind is now again clogged with so many thoughts of the fact that she is being abused, mentally, emotionally, and in all other ways, except physically by his family and him, being no exception to it either. She had also previously on several occasions informed Rajiv that his parents have been directly grumbling and making a fuss about how marriage in their culture does not happen without *'gifts'* in cash and kind.

Amrita told Rajiv, *"If your parents wanted household appliances, furnishings, property and whatnot that they have been telling me about, why didn't they convey this to my parents before marriage? I wouldn't have been here, Rajiv!"*

He then blatantly refuses any such thing happening at all.

Amrita emphatically retaliates, *"Emotional abuse is one of the hardest forms of abuse to recognise. It can be subtle and insidious, overt and manipulative. Either way, it chips away at the victim's self-esteem and they begin to doubt their perceptions and reality, and this is exactly what you are doing, Rajiv, and precisely how I'm feeling. Rather all of you are doing that to me. You are all putting me in a corner and trying to manipulate the reality in my eyes! Shame on you!"*

Amrita looks at the yellow light, the blue-coloured heater in the room and thanks herself for having spoken these lines, aloud, unintentionally. Had she not, she would have already started to feel as if she were crazy. As if she were not able to perceive situations in their true essence. She started to question her own understanding and reasoning of each happening.

Amrita gasps and starts telling him, *"Do you remember how you came to meet me just before our wedding, that warm kiss in the front seat of your parked car?"*

It was more like a defence mechanism. She abruptly wanted to stop thinking and talking about what all is not seemingly right and wanted to remember the good times. She wanted to feel hopeful.

To which Rajiv harshly replied, *"Yes, I do. I also remember how you shooed me away, one day before our wedding from another parking lot where the wedding arrangements were taking place. I also remember how you accused my innocent, old mother of insulting you, right before the ceremonies. I do not understand how you can't see your own behaviour. I don't understand what more we can do for you to act like a 'normal' new daughter-in-law. I don't understand how you can keep on ranting about how unhappy you are. I'm slogging here, working hard to raise the standards of my family and all you do, all day is talk about your own mental problems. You know what? I'm actually sick of you!"*

Amrita is outright in shock. She says from the other side of the phone, her voice cracking, wiping her tears as she chokes. She laughs at her foolishness of trusting someone with her life, not sure whether to care a damn or flow into the pool of emotions she's feeling. She's not sure if she should stand up against or fall prey to this manipulation, not clear if she has already been gaslit. She says, *"You know what is normal?*

Normal is when a husband leaves on the eighteenth day of being married, he either makes arrangements for his wife to travel along or at least soon after. Do you know what else is normal? It's normal for the groom's family to welcome the daughter-in-law, accept her as a human, accommodate her in their lives, house, and family, and not disrespect her. They should not deny validating her feelings, talk ill about her upbringing, refuse to acknowledge her needs, expect her to not have emotions, and to top it all, expect compliant slavery from her."

"I'll tell you what else is normal," Amrita flared. *"You know I left my job, my house, my family, my city for you, to build a home, a life with you, in a whole different part of the country. You know I'm technically, as your wife, financially dependent on you at this very moment. Not like I want your money, but you could have at least offered or asked if I needed anything. Instead, you chose to rather not bother, while on the other hand, you left a few bundles of money for your parents. Normal is when you would make me comfortable, so that we could create a conducive environment to share our thoughts and feelings. What is normal for a husband is to tell his wife all this! Now that's normal, and sadly, neither you nor your people are anywhere even close to this."*

Rajiv, now raging with anger, fulminating, says, *"Keep all these stories of yours to yourself. I do not have time for this pseudo-rebellious attitude of yours. Utterly useless, fictional, TV serial expectations! I have a long day ahead tomorrow and I need to get some sleep."*

He flagrantly disconnects the call.

Amrita's humiliated again, unable to bear the continual disrespect, her quavering voice mumbles, *"Domestic violence is not only always physical, it is also verbal, emotional, financial and EXISTENTIAL."*

She falls asleep crying, feeling and concluding that *"Not all marriages are rosy and romantic, some are otherwise and mine is the latter!"*

How has emotional abuse affected your view of yourself and your relationships? How soon could you recognise it?

FOURTH STITCH

The Fragmented Mind

By Sarab Kaur

"You are worthless, Sia! You make things difficult for me!" screams her exhausted mother. Sia, 11 years old and often called a *"daydreamer"* by some of her friends, got lower marks for her math test, although she prepared thoroughly. Then, what really was the problem? She was an attentive student and a very well-mannered one indeed. *'Something is not right. I have to speak to her teacher,'* thought the overworked mother.

Ignoring her mother's comments, Sia runs towards her grandmother. *"Naani, Naani! Where is my kheer?"* yelled Sia in an irritated tone. *"You promised me you would make me my special kheer! You know it has magic and it's like 'good luck' before my science test!"*

"Oho Sia, I forgot to make it today. How about after your test? When you come back from school, I will have it ready for you. A fresh warm bowl of kheer for my favourite granddaughter." Swiftly moving her hand over Sia's head, arranging the fringes perfectly on point to her eyebrows, *"I'll make a very special one, with extra kesar,"* humbly smiled Sia's grandmother.

Looking at her grandmother, confused and excited, Sia says, *"Ok, but what if I fail? The magic may not work after my test, Naani!"* Grandmother looked at Sia with love and explained to her how there is magic within each one of us and the *'sweet rice pudding'* - the kheer - is merely a belief for any special occasion. Sia suddenly felt powerful and overconfident. It was as if she instantly believed she had magic inside her and would not need to work as hard as other students; getting good grades would surely come easily to her.

Jumping with joy, she leaves for her school. Hopping into the back seat of her fancy little car that her parents have kept especially for her school routine. She shuts the car door, humming her favourite tune. She says with pride, *"Let's go, driver uncle. I don't want to be late, I have a test today and I also have magic in me that will get me good grades."* The driver looked at her via the rearview mirror and smiled. *"Challo, bacha. (Let's go, kiddo)."* He starts the car and whoosh, they're off to school.

As the teacher approached the classroom, students were going through their textbook for a last-minute revision before the test began, and some of them were whispering the answers, trying to memorise them. But Sia, being Sia, was organising her desk; she was all set for the test. She was in a great mood today.

Sia thought to herself, *'I have magic within me, nothing can go wrong!'*

The teacher entered the classroom, greeted the students, and started the test. All the kids nervously started reading the paper and began writing. Here, Sia was in a different dreamland. She browsed the paper with ease and began writing. All the answers that she was writing, she knew some of them were wrong yet didn't bother; she kept repeating to herself, *"I have magic, everything'll be ok."*

She submitted her paper with confidence and left for home. As she walked towards the exit gate, she spotted her car waiting right outside. She looked at her driver and said, *"Driver uncle, let's go home as quickly as possible. Naani promised me kheer today, and I am craving it."*

The driver did not respond to her at all. Sia thought to herself that the driver uncle must be in a bad mood. She shrugged her shoulders, ignored him, and hummed her favourite song again.

Sia imagined the sweet rice pudding, how it was already ready and waiting for her at home. Her Naani even promised that this time she would add some extra kesar strands and pistachios, which were her favourite.

As she enters home, she sees many people weeping and notices her mom crying. She was hungry and craving a fresh bowl of kheer but was greeted with sad faces and teary eyes. Some of them were staring at her with pity, while some treated her as a child who was just interrupting their way towards her mother. Some heavily built aunties unknowingly pushed her aside.

The curiosity led her to wonder what was wrong. Looking around, she noticed a large group of people gathered around her mother. Sia threw her school bag on the floor and ran towards her mother and asked, *"Maa! Why are you crying? What happened?"*

Upon hearing this, her mother began crying even louder. Sia got nervous and was very confused. Looking for her father, Sia ran around the house. She couldn't find him anywhere. She started wondering if something wrong had happened to him. Her father, her uncles, and grandmother were missing. She saw her neighbours gathered at the doorstep, so she pulled up some courage and softly asked a lady, *"Aunty, what happened? Where are my daddy and Naani? I cannot even find my Raj uncle?"* The rude neighbour said, *"Shh, I don't know."* and looked away.

Sia quietly ran into her room and rushed into her bathroom. She stood in front of the bathroom mirror; her panicky breath was fogging up the mirror in front of her. As she wiped the condensation away, the blurred reflection slowly transformed.

Instead of her own face, she saw Naani's kind, familiar eyes gazing back at her. The shock sent a shiver down her spine, but the warmth in those eyes quickly soothed her.

"Sia, beta," her Naani's gentle voice echoed in the small space, *"I know you're feeling anxious right now."*

Sia's eyes filled with tears. *"Naani, is that really you?"*

Her Naani's reflection smiled tenderly. *"Yes, my dear. Remember what I taught you about calming your mind?"*

Sia nodded, her voice trembling. *"Breathe deeply and count to ten."*

"That's right," her Naani said, her tone soothing. *"Close your eyes, take a deep breath in, and slowly let it out."*

Sia closed her eyes and did as instructed. She felt a wave of calm wash over her. She opened her eyes only to realise that it was her and not Naani in the mirror's reflection.

She sat on the bed, still panicking and taking deep breaths. Sia and her Naani are best friends. They make sweet dishes and rangolis together.

While taking deep breaths, she spotted her uncle Raj from the window. She ran downstairs and hugged him. She frantically asked, *"What's the matter, Uncle Raj? Why is everyone sad? Where is Papa?"*

Uncle Raj gave Sia a pitiful smile and told her not to worry, everything will be fine and continued his work. He was greeting the people by folding his hands together, his head bowed down as they were offering condolences. By this time, Sia understood that something bad had happened, but to whom?

Wondering to herself, *"Why is Papa not around? Where is he? Why is Maa crying too much and why did uncle Raj say 'everything'll be fine'?"*

There were so many questions running through her mind. She walked into the kitchen seeking Naani, or if not Naani, at least the kheer would be right there. She looked around and noticed the kadhai on the gas stove with half-cooked rice; it wasn't ready yet. Maybe Naani got busy with all these people gathering, so she must have forgotten to cook it. Sia sighed and picked up a banana, as she was starving.

She looked around hoping to catch a glimpse of either of her two beloved people in the house, her father and her Naani. But both were missing, and she was clueless about what had happened.

Suddenly she heard a voice, *"Well, it is in the hands of God; we are only puppets."*

Those words struck her with grief.

By the time Sia could be reached, they were interrupted by other people who were offering condolences. Noticing how she was sitting on the kitchen table all by herself holding the banana peel in her hand, staring at the kheer uncooked, left on the stove, probably wondering when it would be ready, Sia was found.

The reunion was absolutely spectacular. Sia was relieved to see one of her favourites hale and hearty; she hugged tightly, and the first thing she asked was, *"Why is maa crying? Why are all these people here? And please tell me why this kheer is uncooked? I was promised that I'd be served with my favourite pistachios and kesar."*

She was assured that all of her questions would be answered, but before that, she needs to know something. Something she never thought would occur.

"Sia, your Naani is not with us anymore. She has left for heaven, and all of this happened while you were at school." Sia couldn't imagine what her father was saying.

Those words were misty. They aren't making any sense to her. She could not understand or never realised that Naani could ever be so old to die so soon?

'Was she too old? Or did someone kill her? Why wasn't I there when she wasn't feeling well?' Sia's misty mind got flooded with so many thoughts, and those voices kept echoing in her mind. Her father shook her with bolder words: *"SIA, listen to me! Naani is no more, and she was feeling uneasy; she died because of a heart attack. You need to be calm and go to your room; I'll send some lunch for you."*

"Naani is no more," breathing heavily, *"Naani is... No more..."* Sia kept repeating to herself all the way to her room. She felt faint and light-headed. She couldn't believe this was happening.

She looked at her and Naani's photograph that was pinned under a magnet on the stainless steel almirah and asked, *"But you said I have magic, and that everything will be okay. Did I take all your magic and put it into my science test? Is that why you died?"*

Feeling the guilt rush and absorbing the news, she sits down on the floor, resting her back on the wardrobe Naani and Sia shared. She kept struggling to breathe and tried to control it with the breathing technique taught by her Naani. She looked around; her Naani's simple dark green saree was still wet, that she washed in the morning after her bath. The fragrance and ashes from the agarbatti- incense sticks- were still fresh and aromatic. Sia could not understand how to process this news. It was the very first time she had lost a roommate, her best friend, her grandmother.

As time passed, Sia grew weaker and weaker in her studies and was mostly found lost in her thoughts. A bright, chirpy girl had become dull and cloudy-minded. She hated kheer and never liked the incense sticks anymore. The hatred for her favourite subject, Science, grew stronger and had lost all the magic, the magic her Naani said she had in her.

She grew up to learn that the magic wasn't in the kheer or within her, ever.

It was in the eyes of her Naani, the faith she had in Sia.

The powerful belief she passed on to Sia saying, *"Everything'll be OKAY."*

The ritual of eating the special rice pudding right before the tests or exams was long gone, and the magic faded away, leaving behind the fragmented mind.

Have you lost someone in your life and lost the magic too?

Have you found it yet?

FIFTH STITCH

The Chrysalis Effect

By Sneha Singh

Anish looked at the taxi driver and asked his father, *"Dad, what is uncle drinking from that small earthen pot? Can we also get small pots like those?"*

Anish's father laughed and said, *"That's called a 'Kulad' beta. He's sipping his Chai from it!"*

Anish could not understand, *"Why in the earthen pot though? And why did the man leave that sweet little pot on the side and just zoom away like that?"*

While he was still wondering, they reached their new apartment.

As a nine-year-old, Anish stepped into his new surroundings in Kolkata, and a whirlwind of emotions engulfed his young heart. Leaving behind the bustling streets of Mumbai, he found himself in a city that felt simultaneously familiar and alien. Familiar because he ascertained to his mother, *"The rains are like it used to be in Mumbai, Ma!"*

Soon, excitement mingled with apprehension as he prepared for his first day at the new school. The unfamiliar faces and unknown corridors made him feel like a tiny fish in a vast ocean. Nervously clutching his schoolbag, he found himself in the spotlight. He reminded himself, *"Keep walking, Anish. You are new, and you are not in uniform, so you ought to look like the odd boy out!"*

Anish longed for the comfort of his old friends and the security of his Mumbai routine.

He told his mother, *"Ma, I still cannot believe that we are not in Mumbai anymore; this feels strange. If I had been going to my school in Mumbai, I would have moved to the morning shift this year."*

Anish kept harping on while playing with Brinda, trying to make her hair into a ponytail that sprang up like a water fountain. Anish and his mother giggled at how cute that seemed. Anish's mother called on both her children, *"Come on, let's click some pictures, sit here, Anish and Brinda!"*

With each passing day, Anish and his family would gradually embrace their new environment, weaving their own new world of memories and finding their place in this enchanting city of joy.

Yet, beneath the surface Anish had his share of apprehensions: a new school, a new environment, a new city, a new home, and new surroundings. It was all very brand new for Anish. He, more often than not, told his parents, *"The streets of Kolkata are vibrant although they feel very different."* This was all he could understand and infer at his 9/10 years of age. From all that he got to explore through his new friendships at school and in the colony and through some delightful observational discoveries.

His little sister, Brinda, was very young to understand any of what was happening. It was soon after her first birthday that they had moved to these new surroundings, different from everything that was.

This was all very new not only for Anish but for his parents as well. Anish's father was trying to adapt to his new office and colleagues at work. Even though this was a transfer, because of which Anish's father had to move with his family, he always told his wife how unfamiliar all of it is from one place to another.

"It changes with the culture," he would express. *"Every city has a different feel to it, the way it functions is different*

and the way people behave is, on the surface level, dependent on where they live!" she replied to her husband.

"Moving from Mumbai to Kolkata is a big cultural change for the entire family, my dear," she added.

While, on the other hand, Anish's mother was struggling to work her way with the groceries and the household chores. From finding the nearest supermarket to striking a chord with the house help, from setting up their new company quarters to managing a little 14-month-old child, all by herself, single-handedly. Anish & Brinda, although not very aware of all that their parents were dealing with, had their own share of newbies to handle.

Anish was out playing throwball with his new friends at the colony garden one day when he keenly noticed his mother walking through the gate with heavy bags full of groceries and household essentials in both her hands and Brinda in the baby bag across herself. Anish and Brinda's mother did not know that Anish had noticed this while playing.

Anish mentioned nothing to his mother until the next time, a couple of days later, when his mother again prepared to head out for the supermarket and grocery shopping.

Anish picked Brinda up in his little arms and told his mother, *"Go, Ma, fetch our groceries, I'll forever take care of Brinda."*

It filled Anish's mother with more joy than anything else to imagine that she could have both her hands free and pick all that she desires without having to hold her, now, 16-month-old Brinda in her arms along with the bags. She bid adieu to the kids and left for her stint at the market.

Brinda was young, but Anish was no biggie himself. He was all of 10 who had now started to struggle to lift his baby sister, Brinda. He would carry her down with him to go and play tennis, his favourite game, with his friends. Anish was also still learning how to ride a big bicycle on the road outside the colony lanes. He loved his rugged-wheeled bicycle.

Anish had fond memories of his mother getting it for him on a bright, sunny afternoon, and how the wide, empty street of their colony back in Mumbai beckoned him to take his first solo ride.

Cut to the present day, learning to ride the bicycle without the safety net of a known road, on a real road outside the colony, had always brought a whirlwind of emotions swirling within Anish's mind. He would think to himself, *"As much as I want to ride the bicycle outside, what if I fail? What if I fall? What if Brinda is scared to sit alone on the bench if I leave her there while I go take a ride and come back? What if I take her with me and drop her too? Am I capable enough not to make us fall?"*

Anish could not understand how he could create a balance between taking care of his little sister, his new surroundings, and his yearning for the exhilarating feeling of freedom and accomplishment that would come with riding solo on the real roads.

His newfound colony friends sometimes teased him, saying he had not learnt how to ride the bicycle on his own outside the safe lanes yet. Anish did feel conscious of this and refrained from cycling altogether in the next couple of days.

Over a period of weeks, even when their mother was home and around, Anish tagged Brinda along when he would head downstairs to play. This was their usual routine. Taking care of and nurturing Brinda was inherently a natural instinct for Anish. He would lift Brinda in his arms and play hide and seek with his friends, and while enjoying his tennis game, he would make Brinda sit on the bench beside the court.

In the meantime, Brinda made a friend of her size and age, Rohan. Rohan lived two buildings away, in the same colony as Anish and Brinda. He came out to play with his aunt. Brinda and Rohan built a bond without words.

Anish and Rohan's aunts talked to each other and built their own bond, while Anish and Brinda's aunt would come to visit them – with spoken words, very unlike Brinda and Rohan.

Days passed to become months, and months soon became years. The day had arrived when it was Brinda's first day at school. Anish gasped, *"Oh dear! Brinda, you are a big girl now, aren't you?! Ready for the first day at school?"*

Anish, along with his parents, went to drop Brinda off at school. It was such a remarkable day when the little child, who was always in their arms, was ready to walk into her first-ever classroom. Brinda did so more happily than Anish and her parents had ever thought. Brinda waved goodbye to them and started playing with the other children and toys around her.

Slowly, Brinda grew into a bright student and secured 1st rank in her 1st-grade final exams. Brinda's family was so proud of her. She had turned into this very confident and bold child for whom no stumbling block was a hurdle.

Brinda was now a precocious and ambitious child. She was determined to make a name for herself in the world and achieve great things.

One night when Anish was packing his school bag as usual, he overheard Brinda thoughtlessly say to their cousins, who were visiting them for a family function, *"I know Bhaiya is jealous of me because I get better grades than him!"*

Anish's unanticipated expression was not readable. He took a pause to let the statement sink in and stopped the physical activity of packing his books for the next day. In a dumbfoundedly calm tone, he said, *"Why would I ever be jealous of you, Brinda? You are my baby sister; you have almost grown in my arms. I can never feel that way about you."* Saying so, he smiled at Brinda and his cousins and continued his activity.

Although these words stayed with Anish throughout, and he kept thinking to himself, *"Why does she think like that about me? I honestly don't even know what jealousy could feel like. I understand the dictionary meaning of the word, but I do not think I could feel that for anyone, leave alone Brinda!"*

It lingered in Anish's heart and mind; he kept spiralling, *"How could Brinda ever think of something like that? How could such a small child think and feel like that?"* Needless to say, Anish was not a grown adult himself; he was, after all, still a child.

Years passed, and Brinda came along as one of the brightest kids of her age, becoming more assertive and fearless with each passing year.

Anish, on the other hand, had come along as someone who was struggling with his grades, despite being a bright student. He often got to hear statements like, *"Oh, so Brinda is the first ranker amongst the two of you!"* or *"Anish, look at other kids, they are thinking about how they can get higher grades!"* or *"It's getting late, Anish, you should also now start to take part in more extracurricular activities."* and so on.

Anish always felt responsible towards his parents and Brinda. Taking Brinda to summer camps, filling in for his parents at Brinda's PTAs, actively participating in where Brinda will apply, where she has to go to write her entrance exams, wherever his parents needed him and so on, were the major roles of Anish's life.

"Brinda, oh God! When did you grow up so much that we are now coming to drop you off for your college entrance exams, wow!!" Anish and his mother commented while driving Brinda to the exam centre.

"You have worked hard to secure a seat for yourself in the best possible college, Brinda. You have struggled and worked day in and out to crack the not-so-easy entrance exams. Give it your best shot! Good luck!" the mother and son duo said as they dropped Brinda off.

Soon, the day arrived when Brinda had to leave home and move to another city and consequently to another country.

For Anish and his parents, Brinda's journey was an inspiring one.

Anish in the process became a spectator to happenings of life and the changes he saw in Brinda. He saw her turn into this young girl, full of aspirations, competitive enough to withstand the fast pace of life.

Anish and his parents would, time and again, discuss amongst themselves, *"Brinda has turned into this fine young girl who can travel to places on her own, manage her laundry, her finances, her hostel room. It's wonderful to see her grow into this person,"* his parents would delightfully comment.

Anish reckoned, *"Brinda moved into an apartment all by herself, Dad. Isn't that incredible? Brinda is an adult now. With her own thoughts, ideas, and ways of carrying herself. She has grown and become more successful in her endeavours. She excelled in school, earning top grades and numerous awards, and even in the corporate world as of now!"*

Still in the spectator role, Anish cheered for Brinda and everyone around whenever possible. Encouraging Brinda to pursue her dreams and hobbies while finding himself doing fairly well with his life. Although Anish struggled to find success, despite his efforts, life seemed to always present Anish with challenges, and he had yet to achieve the level of success he desired and deserved. Success was not Anish's friend, let alone being Anish's best friend.

Anish's and Brinda's paternal aunt was visiting their family. She advised Anish, *"Anish, look at Brinda, and for that matter even your cousins. They are all engineers. Even if you aren't one, you're an MBA. Why don't you look for a suitable corporate job for yourself, like them? What will you get by being a lecturer all your life? It will also increase your prospects of finding your perfect princess."* Everyone in the room chuckled and left it at that.

Anish had his share of troubles, and he tried to navigate himself through, but his was a shadowed story. He knew this and was well in acceptance of it. Although he was a bright student, he wasn't among the first few rankers. He was a postgraduate but couldn't find himself the best of jobs. He was living through his bit, as happily as he could, despite not meeting the very expected goals and expectations.

"Success is not for everyone and nothing succeeds like success, Ma. Yes, I agree, but you know what, nothing is as charming as finding the beauty in the ordinary. Also, Ma, accepting one's academic credits as the sole worth of a person isn't really fair, and no one, sadly, sees it that way!" he would often speak his mind to his mother. It wasn't like he had, in all this process, forgotten little Brinda's thoughts when she felt that Anish was envious of her. But he took it with a pinch of salt, *"each to their own!"* he would think to himself.

Anish seldom spoke to himself, *"No, I'm not envious of you, my little child. I'm not envious of anyone for that matter. We're all walking our own path, independent of each other," "Although I do realise that Brinda and I are siblings born to the same set of parents, raised the same way, but Brinda has made her parents proud through her achievements. I am equally proud of that little girl turning into this top-level executive in the corporate world. Being able to manage her workout routine, her growth, her finances and everything quite well. I, on the other hand, have not really made that sort of mark to make my parents proud as such. But I have other aspects that my parents are proud of me for, I'm sure, and there is no comparison, yes, of course, but what is a matter of fact remains a matter of fact. Even if we do not acknowledge it vocally."*

Anish spoke to his friend Mukund, at times, *"Growing up in the shadow of a remarkably successful sibling, my thoughts as the unavailed, not so successful, of the two siblings, have now become a complex interplay of admiration, awe, and a constant struggle to find my own identity."*

"From a very young age, I was exposed to the achievements and accolades garnered by my accomplished sibling, Brinda, and while I genuinely admire Brinda's capabilities, a part of me can't help but wonder what I did or did not do that I haven't reached half of where I could have with the intellect and capabilities I was gifted with," Anish continued speaking his mind.

Mukund pondered and said, *"It seems as though your sibling's achievements have enveloped your own sense of self."*

What transformations are you currently undergoing, and what do you hope to emerge as?

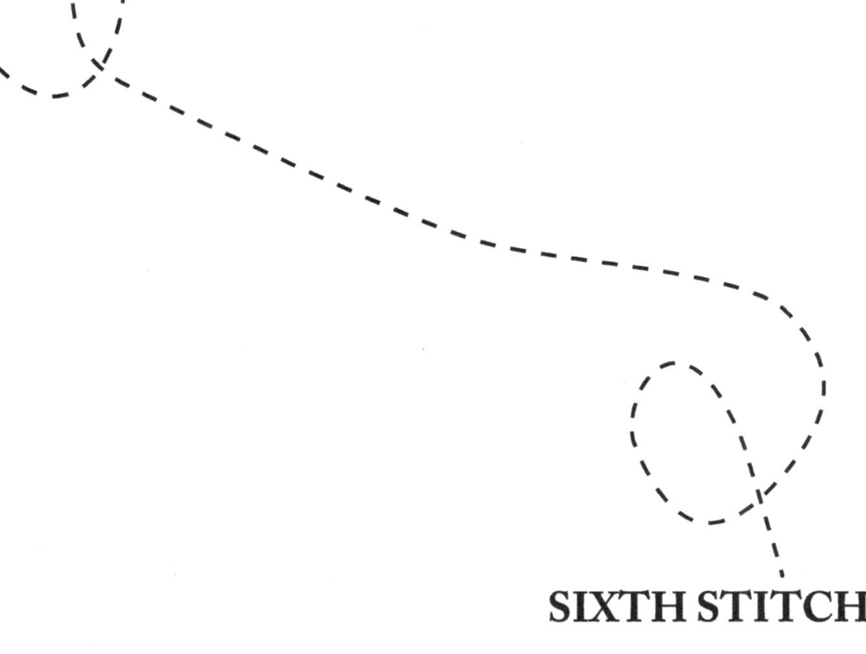

SIXTH STITCH

The Silence Of Truth

By Sarab Kaur

Tap... Tap... Tap... Clicking and clacking sounds of Huda's fingers danced gracefully over the keys of her laptop keyboard as she typed furiously. With each tap, the words on the screen came to life as she captured the emotions of the news story she was covering. She focused on completing her task and thought to herself, *"I need to get this news approved and aired as soon as possible. The terrified family's voice needs to reach thousands of people!"*

As a deaf journalist, she had adapted to using her other senses to navigate the world of reporting, but it had not always been a simple journey. One of many challenges was communicating with people over the phone. She couldn't hear them, so she had to find other ways to get information. Huda learnt to rely on emails, text messages, and face-to-face interviews instead. Sometimes she had to think twice, remembering what the local family had requested of her. Her understanding of what was going on by reading lips was difficult, and she felt really confused about the whole thing. After completing the initial draft, Huda reviewed her report carefully, checking for any errors or inconsistencies. She made revisions as needed to improve clarity.

Huda submitted her report to the editor for review. It took time and patience, but she found her own way to sort things out. As she left her editor's office, she couldn't shake a heavy feeling that settled in her chest. Despite finishing her work, she felt a deep sadness creeping in. Thoughts of her loneliness weighed heavily on her mind, especially regarding her relationship with her husband. She couldn't ignore the growing gap between them, and it left her feeling empty and unsure about their future together. And that's when she felt completely numb.

She walked towards her desk. *'Sigh'* she thought to herself, *"Why do I feel so lost? Everything was perfect and everything seems to be perfect too, except the spark. There is no spark left in our relationship, and I'm not sure if I should feel lonely or not."*

Weighing her options, she tried to deal with what she was feeling. Huda attempted to resolve issues between her and her husband, but nothing seemed to have changed. She sat down on her comfortable chair, nodded her head, and stared at the other pending reports on her laptop screen. She continued to type, bashing the tips of her fingers furiously.

Her marriage to Farhan was once filled with love and understanding, but as the years passed, their connection frayed. There were no more jokes, laughter, or joy. There were misunderstandings and resentments. It wasn't only about the same old everyday stuff anymore. Huda wanted more. She wanted moments that made her feel alive, that really connected with her deep down. As she searched for this, she couldn't ignore the little voice inside her, pushing her to try new things and see what's out there.

She sat alone in the quiet of her bedroom, gazed out of the window into the dark night, her reflection appearing faintly against the glass. The windowsill, dimly lit by the soft glow of a nearby lamp, provided a subtle contrast to the darkness outside. Beyond the window, the night sky stretched endlessly, yet she could only observe the twinkling car lights passing by on the busy highway. She could still see herself faintly in the window, giving her a moment to ponder.

She questioned her place in the marriage, unsure of where she stood and what her role meant to her and her husband. During her emotional contemplation, her mind raced with a series of events where the question arises as to the what ifs and what nots. Huda asked herself, *"Where do I fit in this marriage? Am I truly seen and valued for who I am, or have I become a mere reflection of my husband's expectations? Am I sacrificing too much of myself for the sake of our relationship?"*

With each passing moment, Huda's self-reflection led her to question the depth of understanding and communication she shared with her husband. She overthought every minor incident, the conversations, and those petty fights that took place repeatedly. She kept asking herself these vague questions. *"I may be deaf and mute but my heart screams louder than ever! Is my voice being heard? Are my needs and emotions being acknowledged or even respected? Or have they become secondary to maintaining the status quo?"*

Days passed, and nothing had changed.

One fateful day, when Huda was at work in a busy news station studio. Her mind was preoccupied with the turmoil in her personal life, and her hands were full of files and paperwork. She noticed everyone being busy on phone calls and setups, dodging the crowd and wires. As she walked towards her cubicle, lost in her thoughts, she collided with a man.

When Huda and Akash bumped into each other, there was a soft thud as they collided. Papers fluttered to the ground, making a rustling sound, and pens clattered against the desk. In the busy office where phones rang and people chatted, creating a constant buzz, Huda, being deaf and unable to speak, couldn't hear any of it. She only felt the bump and saw the papers flying, while Akash's sudden movement startled her.

Despite the lack of noise, the collision made her aware of the hustling world around her. Akash, a charming and humorous accountant who might have seemed to find a moment in the chaotic environment of the studio. Their eyes met, and it seemed like two lost birds had found what they were seeking.

Few seconds of a stare and Akash broke out the words, saying, *"Oh! I am so sorry, miss. I hope I didn't hurt you."*

Unaware of Huda's deafness, Akash engaged in a lively conversation, not realising that she couldn't hear his words. Huda wanted to stop him right there, to tell him she could not hear a word, but she could see how rapidly his lips were moving and how his eyes met hers. After a point, Akash stopped talking, confused to see why she hadn't responded yet.

Akash mumbled to himself, *"Is she even interested?"* He quickly apologised one last time and escaped from there. Huda simply understood why he ran away after mumbling and hence to clear the misunderstanding and to start off on a better note, Huda started and wrote him a note, stating the fact of her being deaf and that she didn't mean to scare him away. She handed over the note to him personally while they were exiting the office. When Akash got the note, he read it immediately, widened his eyes, looked at her with an embarrassed smile, held his earlobe with his right hand, and moved his lips to sync with the word *"SORRY"*.

They both smiled together and walked out of the building in silence.

For a few days, a couple of warm smiles were exchanged as they crossed each other's desks at work. In the meantime, Akash wanted to understand Huda better, so he learnt sign language to communicate with her. His first step was to look up tutorials on YouTube that would teach him what he needed to know. Every day, he would watch the videos and practice the signs. He learnt a few signs and gestures and was eager to communicate.

He hoped to build a connection with her, proving that he tried learning sign language, just for her. Akash realised he was being drawn to Huda differently; it was a different *'something special.'* He looked forward to seeing her in the mornings, waiting for her at the entrance of the building, pretending to be on calls or checking emails.

The weekends made him feel low, as he couldn't meet her in person. Huda was slowly becoming someone special to him; she was not just an office colleague anymore. She often felt his vibe. She knew nothing about him and showed less interest as she was already in a marriage full of complications. Despite all well-thought morals and logics, she still couldn't control the urge of knowing Akash more.

One morning in the office cafeteria, Akash approaches Huda with a warm smile, his hands moving gracefully to form the signs. He taps his hand to ask *"can,"* then points to himself for *"I."* With a gentle motion, he pretends to stir something in his hand for *"make,"* before pointing to Huda for *"you."* Finally, he completes the gesture by making a circular motion to signify *"coffee."* His sign language said, *"Can I make you a cup of coffee today?"*

Huda is surprised and has a big smile on her face. She gently nodded her head and gave him a thumbs up. Soon, this became a daily ritual. They started noticing the time of each other's coffee breaks, and then it suddenly became their quiet coffee break.

A few weeks later, one evening in the cafeteria, Huda takes out her phone and types a note, *"care to exchange numbers?"* Then, she shows it to Akash with a smile. Understanding her gesture, Akash nods and quickly saves his number on her phone. He hands it back to Huda, who then thanks him with a grateful smile. With his number safely stored in her phone, Huda felt a sense of excitement about staying connected with Akash. They had quite frequent chats. One day, Akash couldn't hold his words back and finally summoned the courage to type what he really felt.

-Messages-

Akash: Good evening, Huda! I've been meaning to ask you this for a very long time. Is it just me, or does the world seem a little brighter when you're around?

Huda: Well, hello there, Akash! I must admit, your charming words have a way of making me blush. I guess my world seems to be brighter too, with your presence around me. Does that answer your question? Otherwise, how's your day been treating you?

Akash: My day was ordinary until this very moment when I had the pleasure of receiving an instant reply to my question. And of course, days have become brighter and brighter since I've crossed paths with you. Suddenly, everything feels extraordinary. You have that effect on me.

Huda: Oh! Is it! Haha! Well, you know just the right words to make my heart skip a beat!

As Akash and Huda continued their flirty chat, the connection they had developed fascinated them. The possibility of a blossoming romance excited them. Being around Akash, the weight of her troubled marriage momentarily lifted. There was an unspoken connection between them, a comfort that Huda hadn't felt in years. They spent more time together and discovered a lot in common.

It was during one of their late-night chats that Huda opened up about her troubled marriage. Their connection deepened, the lines between friendship and something more blurred.

Huda found happiness in Akash's presence; his humour and understanding became a balm for her troubled heart. But as their relationship teetered on the edge of forbidden territory, guilt gnawed at Huda's conscience. She went into the flashback of the moments she had with her husband and realised what she was doing was morally wrong. She had already taken steps to complicate things further between her and Farhan, whereas she should've been easing things out.

She stood by the same window of her bedroom, staring at her reflection, this time a bit of a blurry sight as it was pouring heavily. This time the questions were on the weight of guilt that settled heavily on her shoulders. She found herself engaged in a deep conversation with her conscience, filled with the emotions and doubts that had been plaguing her.

Huda, (whispering to herself in her mind) *What have I done? How did I allow myself to get swept away in this whirlwind of emotions? I feel so guilty, as if I've betrayed the trust and love that my husband has given me.*

Her conscience responded, urging her to confront the reality and the impact it could have on her marriage.

> *Conscience: Huda, you know deep down that what you're feeling is a breach of trust. Even though you found a ray of hope that was refreshing for you, yet based on moral grounds of respect, your husband deserves your loyalty and commitment. It's time to confront your guilt and accept the consequences.*
>
> *Huda: I know, I know. I can't ignore the fact that I've allowed myself to be entangled in this situation. I've jeopardised the foundation of our marriage, and it tears me apart.*

Conscience: Remember the love and bond you share with your husband? Are you willing to bear the consequences of your actions not only for yourself but for the family you've built together? Is this fleeting infatuation worth risking everything you hold?

Huda: No, it isn't. My husband is my rock, my confidant, and the father of our children. I need to confront this guilt and make things right. I owe it to him and to our family.

Her conscience gently encouraged her.

Conscience: Huda, it's time! Communicate with Farhan. It's never too late to fix your mistakes. You both can work together to rebuild the trust that has been compromised.

With a heavy heart, Huda messaged Akash on the chat and spoke about the beauty of their relationship. What they found was like a breath of fresh air, although it could not be continued.

-Message-

Huda: Akash, I need to talk to you. Our relationship has been like a beautiful dream, but I'm afraid it's time to wake up. It hurts to say this, but I think we need to go our separate ways. I can't shake this feeling of guilt, and I'm sorry if I've hurt you. Goodbye, and take care.

Akash: Whoa! Wait. What? What do you mean? I thought everything was going well between us. Please don't leave like this. Let's talk it out.

Huda: I wish we could, but I don't think it's the right thing to do. It's better if we part ways now before things get more complicated. I hope you understand.

Akash: I think I understand, but can't it just be the way it is? I have no expectations from you. I know you're having a difficult time in your marriage, but... Can't we work through whatever is bothering you?

Huda: I'm sorry, Akash, but I've decided. This guilt and my conscience keeps pulling me back. I am so sorry to have come into your life, and I genuinely appreciate the time we spent together, but it's best if we say goodbye now.

Akash: Please, Huda, don't do this. I don't want to lose you. How about you take a break? Let's see how it goes? My life hasn't been this comfortable since Alka passed away. Is there anything I can do to change your mind?

Huda: I'm sorry, Akash, but this is goodbye. Take care of yourself.

Huda blocks Akash in the chat, ending their conversation and their short-lived relationship.

Huda realised that going back into the troubled marriage with her guilt could completely ruin it, leaving nothing to salvage. She had a tough conversation with her husband, Farhan. She laid bare her guilt, reasoned her actions, and sought forgiveness. Farhan sat there listening to her, not being able to believe that his trophy wife would betray him. It came as a shock that out of anything else she would find a shoulder to cry on and seek the spark with someone else.

The arguments in sign language and cold shoulder behaviour went on longer than expected. But as days passed, Huda tried to communicate with Farhan and made him realise every aspect of *'that's how'* and *'now what'*. He tried his best to understand the misled steps Huda took and realised he had to apologise as well for the lost spark between them. They both worked on their relationship for the sake of their family.

Akash looked at the display picture on his phone and whispered, *"My child deserves my full presence and love. I gave up my time on him for this fling with Huda. I will never let this happen again."* He then looked up at the sky and the passing clouds and whispered, *"I'm sorry, Alka. I'll do better."* He closed his eyes, took a deep breath, and let go of the distractions that had clouded his mind.

And as time passed, their paths crossed again, this time as friends who had withstood the storm of temptation. They exchanged a knowing glance in the cafeteria, silently acknowledging each other's presence, and carried on making their own cups of coffee. Akash catches Huda's attention; with a concerned expression, he signs, *"All okay with Farhan?"* Huda's heart skips a beat as she meets his gaze. Emotions well up inside her as she signs back, *"Not really. Things are tough."*

A wave of sadness washes over her, knowing that her struggles are visible to Akash, yet grateful for his concern and she signs, *"But they will be better someday."* She walks towards the entrance of the cafeteria with her head down, stops, takes a deep breath, and slowly walks towards her cubicle.

She sits down and stares at her desk. Feeling overwhelmed, she takes a sip of her coffee and tries to focus on her work, but her mind is elsewhere.

What truths have you been afraid to confront, and how might they liberate you?

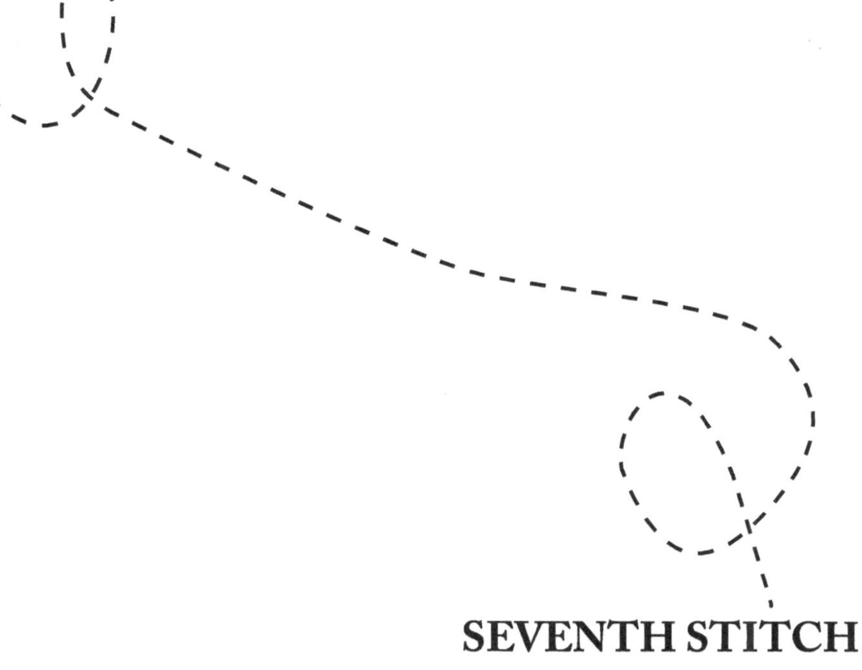

SEVENTH STITCH

The Scent Of Anosmia

By Sneha Singh

Ardaas looked at the big stain running from her shoulders down to her knees and how the gravy was flowing from her hair. No matter how much she cleaned, it was still dripping from her hair, onto her chef's coat and she flared, *"I have my final 'Culinary Arts Display' interview at the Jaivana Palace tomorrow! Argh!!!"*

Kannan looked at her and laughed, *"You look adorable,"* he said.

"No, I do not have another chef's coat for tomorrow. WHAT am I going to do, Kannan?"

Kannan held Ardaas's hand and walked her to the huge mirror in their living room, the gravy still dripping, now slowly, from her hair, and in a pleasing tone, coherently said, *"Meet Ardaas, a determined chef, with an insatiable passion for exploring the unknown, whose heart beats to the rhythm of adventure and learning. What is it that YOU cannot do? You can do it all, my love. It's not your chef's coat that's doing its share at the interview tomorrow. It's you! We'll find a way. Now calm down and focus on what you need to prepare, leave that chef's coat of yours to me."*

The sound of credence in his voice was the most soothing thing for Ardaas in that moment.

In the bustling city of Jaipur, amidst vibrant colours and rich traditions, Ardaas and Kannan were carving their way towards establishing themselves as an individually and professionally successful couple.

Their love story began in the corridors of their high school. They have always been the duo, whose bond exemplifies unwavering support and affection for each other. Ardaas, with her culinary finesse and a heart filled with a passion for gastronomy, had embraced her dream of becoming a renowned chef. Her creative flair in the kitchen knew no bounds. While Kannan, her doting husband, has always been her number one fan and critic at the same time. *"I will always encourage her to reach for the stars. Although I won't flatter her for nothing!"* he would always say.

Meanwhile, Kannan is a talented architect and the visionary behind breathtaking structures that blend modernity with Jaipur's rich cultural heritage. With each brick he lays, Ardaas stands firmly by his side, admiring his dedication and drive. Together, they are an inseparable force, navigating the highs and lows of life with a bond that only deepens with time. Their high school love story had blossomed into an unbreakable partnership, where their individual passions fuel one another, creating a symphony of love and encouragement that resonates through the colourful streets of Jaipur.

Since Ardaas was four, she was fuelled by an insistent, quenchless passion for motorcycles. Girls her age usually asked for dolls and Barbies, but Ardaas went to the toy store only to lay her hands on the most rugged, sometimes agile, and versatile bikes available. Her parents were amused by how such a young child would even have such a sharp sense of what exactly was the difference in all of those bikes. As a child, she would watch shows of women who rode from one part of the country to the other. Ardaas's interest over the years leaned particularly towards the iconic Royal Enfield. She was thirteen when she ran to her parents one day and said, *"Ma, Pa, I dreamt of myself astride a powerful Bullet, the wind ruffling through my hair, and the roar of the engine echoing in my ears."*

Her parents were flabbergasted, noticing the glee in Ardaas's eyes. Their eyes met each other's while she was talking. The glances they exchanged spoke unuttered words that demonstrated mutual feelings of elation.

Ardaas continued speaking with as much enthusiasm in her tone about her lucid dream, *"You know what? In the dream, I wore camouflaged pants and a black t-shirt. My nails were painted with thick, solid black nail polish, and I had a couple of tattoos on my fingers and several silver rings as well."*

Her parents smiled and appreciated her spirit and love for riding. Her mother said to her father, *"Even in her dreams, she is the embodiment of freedom. It perfectly portrays her rebellious spirit."* Her father nodded in agreement.

Ardaas forever followed countless female riders from across the globe on her social media handles, even as a young girl. She would run to her mother more often than not and share the stories of the adventures of these women whom she followed. Their endeavours fuelled her passion even more. She would often turn to her mother, with her eyes filled with determination, and ask, *"When will I be old enough to ride a Bullet 350, just like these amazing women, Ma.. Ma tell me no please.. Maaa tell me?"* She would nag her mother until she had a reconfirming answer each time.

Her mother smiled every single time at her when she asked this question and told her, *"Only after you turn eighteen, my dear. Not a second before that!"*

The moment Ardaas heard this, she would count on her fingers, *"Ma, six more years to go? Ma, five more years to go?"*

Ardaas is an only child. As the years passed, Ardaas's enthusiasm for motorcycles only grew stronger. She counted down the days until her 18th birthday when, finally, she would be legally allowed to ride her own motorcycle. On the eve of her 18th birthday, she couldn't sleep. The anticipation was overwhelming.

She expressed, *"Ma, Pa, from tomorrow onwards I am going to be able to ride, officially!"*

The morning sun broke through her window, and Ardaas sprang out of bed. She couldn't wait any longer. With trembling fingers, she unlocked her phone and frantically scrolled through her Instagram account.

There it was, the answer to her dreams - The Royal Enfield Club that specialised in teaching enthusiasts how to ride the legendary Royal Enfield Bullet 350.

Her heart raced as she rushed to her father's room. Bursting with excitement, she pleaded, *"Pa, I found it! I found a club that can teach me how to ride a Bullet 350! Please, can I enrol? It's my 18th birthday gift!"*

Her father always knew how excited she was about this. Seeing the fire in her eyes and the genuineness in her voice, there was no chance he could refuse. He smiled warmly and said, *"Ardaas, you've been dreaming of this for so long, haven't you? Alright, let's make it happen. Happy 18th birthday, my passionate rider."*

He appealed, *"Just promise me, you will always be safe. And never, never will you overspeed and put my child's life in any danger."*

Ardaas and her father smiled and shook hands. She said, *"I promise, Pa, I will!"*

Her mother, smiling from a distance, observed the emotional conversation between the father-daughter duo, clicked a picture of the moment in which they shook hands in agreement.

Ardaas almost felt as if tears would roll off her eyes as she hugged her father tightly. Her dream had finally come within reach, and she was ready to embark on the thrilling journey of learning to ride the Bullet 350. She said, *"Yay, I'm now going to be one among all of those fierce and adventurous women who have inspired me for all these years, from around the world."*

As the days passed, Ardaas's passion burned brighter. She couldn't wait to put on her camouflage pants, black t-shirt, and deck herself with her favourite rings and nail polish. Her Bullet awaited her. She told Kannan, who was a very dear friend of hers by now, *"The Bullet to me feels like a symbol of freedom and adventure, and I have forever determined to make my childhood dream a reality. I know that with the wind through my hair and the roar of the engine, I will become one with the open road. That's just what I have always envisioned."*

Ardaas always said to herself and out loud to everyone, with the most grateful smile on her beaming face, *"How blessed am I to have such supportive parents and friends."*

"My parents and my dearest friends have always accepted me for who I am, my riding and my passion for cooking. I am definitely not even thinking of anything except for a 'Hotel Management' course for what I want from my life."

Years passed by, and now Ardaas had turned twenty-five.

Meet Ardaas, a young woman with a deep passion for her Royal Enfield Bullet. Her love for riding went beyond the ordinary, leading her on extraordinary journeys that amazed everyone. With her Bullet by her side, she ventured into unknown places, tackled rough terrains, and embraced the excitement of the adventure. Ardaas became a symbol of fearless exploration, and her incredible rides turned into stories of a legend. She wasn't just a rider; she was a trailblazer, redefining what was possible on two wheels and inspiring others to pursue their own dreams in the world of motorcycling.

She became one of those whom she looked up to as a child. She had now surpassed them. She came to be known as the *'Rider Chef'* on social media and started receiving acknowledgement for her riding and cooking videos.

Ardaas was approached by various big restaurants. They wanted her to join them as their head chef. She was also getting a lot of attention from the food bloggers who would write articles about her and her journey as a chef and how she managed her biking expeditions, being such a renowned name in the *'Food and Beverage'* industry.

Ardaas had gained popularity from the series in which she would make videos of herself cooking famous dishes from each state in the country along with the dishes that were lesser known, especially street food. She became an internet superstar chef popular among netizens. She would ride to places and explore the streets of India to understand the local food and what cuisine interests the people, record the entire journey, and then cook the recipes she learnt about and shoot that too.

Ardaas had started to be featured in the local newspaper frequently for the street food recipes.

Meanwhile, Ardaas and Kannan tied the knot. Theirs was a minimalist wedding with only their near and dear ones being a part of their ceremony at the Gurudwara. Kannan and Ardaas never really confessed their love for each other. They first became friends when Kannan moved to their school in the seventh grade. He and Ardaas were put in a science project together along with three other members in their team and since then, they were really close and stayed friends.

One fine day on an Instagram live interview, when asked about her marriage plans, Ardaas happened to mention, *"I would want to marry no one but my best friend."*

Kannan later asked her about it, *"What did you mean when you said you will marry your best friend Ardaas?"*

Ardaas chirped, *"I mean marriage should feel simple and at home, right? And who other than my best friend can make me feel like that? I want my marriage to just change my marital status on paper. We support and stand by each other without judgements, only want the best for each other, come what may!"*

Kannan looked at her and said, *"You mean like 'US'?"*

Ardaas blushed and said, *"Wait, what? Ahhh, yeah, actually YES, YES, OMG!!!" "Kannan Batra, will you marry me?"*

Kannan jumped and gushed, *"Of course!"*

They got married a month and a half later.

Fast forward to the present day. Ardaas had her important interview at the Jaivana Palace. They were offering her an irresistible opportunity. She was all prepared, *"Kannan, I am leaving, come on out! Wish me luck!"*

Kannan walked out of the kitchen with a bowl of yoghurt mixed with sugar, *"Hmm, wait up, have this dahi chini first!"* and fed her a spoonful of the sweet mixture. *"What is it you can't achieve? You rode from Kashmir to Kanyakumari on your Bullet 350! Vijay Bhava!" (victory be yours),* Kannan said and bid her adieu.

Ardaas gulped the yoghurt and ran out, *"See you soon, have a lovely day,"* and she rode away, with the engine sounding like the trumpet of victory.

A couple of days into her new role at the Jaivana Palace, life seemed to have left no stone of happiness unturned for Ardaas.

She and Kannan were planning to go to the Rann of Kutch for the upcoming holiday season.

"I'm running really late today, Kannan!" Ardaas said to Kannan over the phone.

"It happens at times, don't rush Aardas!" Kannan prodded.

Ardaas rode away, the sense of urgency making her restless. She honked at everyone on the way. She glanced at her watch while she rode apprehensively, *"I might just make it in time if I cross this flyover in less than three minutes,"* she deliberated and computed with herself, *"A minibus and five cars, a couple of bikes. I can zip, zap, and zoom if I cut slant past the cars and overtake the bus along its right side."*

Ardaas honked frantically and, while trying to overtake the bus, found herself stuck between a car and the bus. She accelerated.

"Do you know who this is?" Ardaas heard a faint voice. She struggled to open her eyes. With her eyes partially open, Ardaas felt she was in a hospital, surrounded by people she knew and a doctor. The nurses were running helter-skelter.

"That is my father," she spoke in a feeble voice. She felt she couldn't open her eyes fully, and her face felt swollen. The doctor bent over, close to her, so he could hear her. *"And can you tell me who this is?"* the doctor asked yet again, pointing in the opposite direction.

Ardaas felt she was struggling to speak. *"My husband,"* she muttered.

The doctor left. Kannan, his parents, Ardaas's parents, and a few close friends were all standing in the hospital lobby.

"What exactly happened, Kannan?" they all asked almost at the same time.

Kannan sighed, *"She was late, I knew. And then I got a call about 35-40 mins later that Ardaas had met with a severe accident and that I needed to rush to this government hospital; she is being brought here!"*

Kannan continued looking at both the fathers and said, *"Someone who saw what happened came along with her to the hospital."*

"Papa," Kannan gasped, sounding worried, *"The lady looked really worried and said Ardaas rammed into the bus and flew over the flyover to fall under it. She fell into a heap*

of crushed stones, the ones used in construction. The lady said Ardaas had lost a lot of blood."

Ardaas's father sat on the bench hearing all this, *"This is all my mistake."*

"She will be fine, Grewal Sahab, please do not think like this," said Kannan's parents. Ardaas's mother nodded in agreement with them.

Kannan, distraught, said, *"They are just doing some basic first aid in this government hospital, let us please shift her to a bigger hospital. She has lost so much blood, she needs to be shifted. I felt her eyes were very non-reactive, Papa, let's please move out of here."*

They moved Ardaas to a larger hospital. It was found that she has suffered a serious internal injury and there's also a clot. She needed to undergo surgery immediately.

The doctor said to them, *"I am going to try my best, but we cannot tell what will be the outcome of such surgery. The clot damages the cells, and what part of the body is controlled by those cells is uncertain. She could lose any part or function of the body. Memory, speech, hearing, a limb, we just cannot tell. Our job is to try, Mr. Batra. In the meantime, all you can do is pray for the best."*

The surgery began. A couple of hours later, the nurses ran out saying, *"She's suffering a paralytic attack, get these injections urgently from the pharmacy downstairs. Please be quick. Real quick!"* the nurse reiterated.

After fourteen hours, the doctor came out of the operation theatre. Kannan and both sets of parents ran towards him, *"How is Ardaas?"* they inquired.

"We have done our best, the surgery went fairly well except for the paralytic attack. We treated it with the medication that was required in between. The next few hours are critical. We just have to wait and watch now. All the best." the doctor affirmed and left.

Eighty-four hours post-surgery, Ardaas gained consciousness. Everyone was worried. There seemed to be no change in her in the last three and a half days. This was in a way good as there were no after-effects, but it was also concerning because a prolonged state of unconsciousness would mean she had slipped into a coma.

After she regained consciousness, the doctors came to check on her, her vitals, and all other necessary checks.

Fifty-three days later, the most awaited day had arrived. Ardaas was going to get discharged. She had made it back to life without losing anything vital. There could have been nothing more than this for her family and friends.

She fought a battle, and so did her family in these almost two months from the day of her accident. Their prayers had all been heard.

A few days after settling at home, her family organised a grand get-together for their near and dear ones to celebrate Ardaas's return, which is nothing short of a miracle. There were very slim chances of her survival and survival with normalcy. This was a comeback from something that nearly took her life. They said, *"Your being with us is a miracle, Ardaas; we must celebrate God's mercies."*

Ardaas got dressed and looked at herself in the mirror, "Kannan, I have lost the hair that I loved most when they would fly with the breeze while I rode. I have also lost my riding for life, no?" she questioned.

This was the first time she had spoken about her riding. *"What happened to my Bullet Kannan?"* she inquired.

"It will all be better, my love. About the Bullet, we sold it, the way it was." Kannan replied without making eye contact.

Avoiding any further conversation around it, Ardaas said, *"I cannot smell you, Kannan,"* saying, so she sprayed her favourite perfume on the inside of her left wrist and said, *"I cannot smell this either!"*

Kannan understood what had happened, but he responded, saying, *"It could be because of the medicines, Ardaas. It will all settle in a while. Now let's get ready and leave. Everyone is waiting out there for us."*

Ardaas, Kannan and their families sat together after the party when everyone had left and were having a light conversation about the evening and the guests. It was a beautiful evening for all of them, like the calm after the storm.

Ardaas said to everyone, *"Where did the food come from? No aroma at all in the food. The taste was excellent, but I just couldn't FEEL it."*

"In fact," she continued, *"I have been feeling that ever since I got home. I cannot smell the tadka in the dal (lentils), I couldn't even smell the oregano when we ordered pizza the other day. My early morning coffee only feels like warm water, with absolutely no aroma of the coffee. I feel really sad. I don't understand what's happening!"*

Both sets of parents looked at Kannan.

"Somebody say something! Why are you all only looking at each other and then looking at Kannan and not saying anything?"

"You were going to lose something, Ardaas. It could have been anything: your sight, your hearing, speech, memory, perhaps a limb. Patients in such cases could become a living vegetable for life. Waheguru ki meher hai (Wonderous Lord's Grace), you are safe and sound, sitting here and sipping this post-party coffee with all of us. That's all that matters. What will we lose if you can't smell things?" Kannan said in a soft tone as he sat beside her and held her close to him as he spoke.

She looked at him with no understanding of what he was saying! She looked at the parents, *"What? I don't understand. What do you mean to say, Kannan?"*

"You have lost your sense of smell, Ardaas. ***Anosmia*** *it is. I know it is a significant loss. The world of scents, the fragrance of flowers, the aroma of your favourite meals - all gone, like a fading dream. It took its hold on you, and I won't pretend it's anything less than a harsh occurrence. Although, beta, there couldn't have been a better deal. Nothing is more important than you recovering from a head injury and a clot in your brain leading to thirty-four stitches on your skull and you still, today, sitting here absolutely normal with us. This is just a chapter in your life which does not define you."* Ardaas's father clarified.

Ardaas remained quiet for a while.

Painfully, she spoke, *"I am the head chef at a five-star hotel. What will I do without the aroma of my food?"*

Silence prevailed in the room.

"So I am neither a rider, nor the perfect chef? Hashtag not a rider chef?" Ardaas said as she got up and picked a frame hung in the living room of their home, in which she stood smiling at the camera, leaned on her Bullet with her helmet between her left arm and waist, as if it were her baby.

Ardaas grieved, *"I obviously cannot ride anymore, something I longed for and loved for all the years of my life. I waited 18 years to be able to ride, only for it to be taken away from me in just 10 years. Is life even fair?"* she said as she glided her fingers on her Bullet in the frame.

Ardaas continued, *"And how will I be the best chef around without being able to smell what I'm cooking? The aroma of food enhances the taste and experience of consuming it. I have lost the satisfaction of cooking and serving."*

"I can't help but feel the weight of fate's cruel hand upon my life. It's as if the universe has conspired to take away the two most important things that ever made me feel whole."

She thought aloud without even taking a breath, *"My heart is aching with the absence of those two pillars that once held up my world. Kannan, they were my constants, the guiding stars in my sky, and now, they're gone, leaving behind a void I'm struggling to comprehend. Why did fate choose me for this cruel twist of destiny? Was it written in the stars that I should bear this heavy burden?"*

***

What memories or experiences have you lost touch with?

How can you rediscover them?

EIGHTH STITCH

The Rainbow Boundaries

By Sarab Kaur

"How have I come to this point? Why has time stood still and why can't I feel like it used to, as years ago!" Jay whispered to himself. He was magnetically drawn back to the time when they were all together, a tight-knit circle of friends. With a subtle twist of his wrist, he gazed at the tattoo.

Tracing the tattoo on his wrist, he remembered how a few years ago while lounging in Varun's apartment, Zoya, the smarty pants, came up with an idea of having matching tattoos that would represent their unbreakable friendship and their extra-famous trio in the whole of college.

Varun excitedly and blindly said yes, and Jay, at the time, having the fear of needles and commitment issues, took his sweet time to say yes to it. Eventually, they got an appointment with the best tattoo artist in the city, and the day arrived. The present moment grew smaller and smaller, and the flashback washed over Jay like a wave, carrying him into a time and place of a little tattoo shop.

"Hey, uh, I guess I'm up next, right?" Jay asked nervously of the tattoo artist.

"Yup, that's right! Don't worry, it's going to be a breeze. Just relax and let me know if you need a break at any point."

"I've never done this before." Jay's fear was not just about the pain; it was also about the permanence, about commitment.

The idea of having something etched onto his skin for the rest of his life was daunting. What if he regretted it later? What if it did not turn out the way he visualised it?

Zoya knew he had a fear of commitment and needles, so she tried to lighten up his inking process with humorous conversations.

The trio got identical tattoos done on their wrists on the same arm, in the same spot.

Zoya was the glue that held the group together. She had convinced the boys to get the compass tattoo and quoted *'this compass represents commitment to each other.'*

Time flew by and the trio donned graduation caps. They celebrated their graduation with a little getaway to a beachside retreat. As the turquoise waves crashed against the shore, they laughed, talked about their college days, and discussed the future.

There was something brewing in Jay's heart for quite some time. He got up and asked, *"Can you join me for a bit?"* With the sun setting in the background and a nervous smile, he straightaway jumped in and confessed, *"I think I am in love with you. I don't want you to feel awkward at all; I just wanted to share my feelings with you."*

Those words hung in the air, building anticipation.

After a couple of years...

"I am trying! I have missed you more! I can't wait to see you as well. Don't be late," replied Jay over the phone. Muffled sounds of laughter, music, and applause from a drag event could be heard in the background. Before Zoya could figure out the subtly filtered sounds, Jay hung up on her.

Jay was returning to India after a couple of years in the UK, as he finished his internship programme. He missed his homeland and, more importantly, his lifelong friends. Zoya wanted to tell Jay how her feelings had only grown stronger over the couple of years.

At the airport, Zoya was waiting for Jay, her heart pounding with anticipation. She wanted to tell him that her feelings had changed and that she was no longer the same Zoya. She took a deep breath and readied herself for the conversation.

"You're here!" Zoya ran into his arms, and he swirled her around. She hugged him tightly around his chest, followed by happy tears. Another voice, sipping on a soda cup, from behind the pillar of the huge airport said, *"You are finally here!"*

Jay turned back and saw Varun standing there, awaiting his turn to meet his best friend after 2 long years, waiting patiently to hug it out. *"Varun! Man, what a surprise! I have missed you so much!"* Varun quietly smiled, nodding his head.

These three friends reunited after two long years. As they sat in the cab, each one was yapping, constantly sharing whatever came to their mind. The cabbie got confused as to whose voice belonged to whom. As they hit the road, Zoya asked them to show their wrists and clicked a picture of their compass tattoos, uploading it on all of their social media handles, quoting, *"#The trio is back."*

Zoya excitedly interrogated, *"Finally, I get to ask you this, eye to eye! Are you still...?"*

Jay, hesitated under pressure, nervously just smiled and changed the topic to the pollution and potholes on the road.

A few days later.

One fine evening, Zoya walked into the living room where she introduced her love of life to her parents with pride. The initial nervousness turned into genuine warmth and acceptance as they saw the happiness this guy brought to Zoya's life. Soon their families connected, they shared stories and laughter over meals.

Varun and Jay had a business plan that they wanted to accomplish. After years of education, training, internship experiences, and working jobs, they decided to start their own company. During their meetings and work, Jay insisted Varun move in for a few months. They were setting up efficient systems and processes and had to work on establishing a strong core team to build a solid business. They sought a villa in co-sharing, seeking the convenience of living closer to their production unit.

However, beneath the surface, a conflict of interest brewed.

Jay wrestled with feelings of insecurity. He noticed the undeniable bond between Varun and Zoya and did not want to disrupt the balance of their friendship and business partnership. Although Jay's internal struggle was complex, he was torn between his emotions and commitments as a friend.

Entering the villa, Jay notices Varun on a video call with Zoya.

"Oh, still on a video call," his tone laced with sarcasm.

Varun didn't realise the tone and replied, *"Yeah.. She has some news to share."*

"Interesting. Carry on." He raised an eyebrow and walked away into his bedroom.

An hour later, Varun called Jay repeatedly, asking him to join for dinner, but Jay didn't respond. So, he went upstairs only to find him staring out of the window, as if hypnotised. Varun kept calling his name, but he didn't reply.

He gave him a sudden jolt to snap out of it.

Jay whispered, *"I can't help but notice a few things, even when my mind asks me to look at the logic but my heart says no."*

"What? What are you talking about?" Varun asked, looking puzzled.

"I don't want to believe it! Believe me, I've tried. I just can't. I felt free in the UK. I could be myself. But here I'm again, coating myself into someone I am not."

With a scrunched-up face in confusion, Varun replied, *"I really don't know what you are talking about, buddy?"*

Jay looks at him with disappointment. He nods his head, picks up his phone, and stares at a few pictures.

Varun and Zoya were closer than ever, and Jay could not ignore the signs – the lingering glances, the whispered conversations made him upset.

He realised they had found comfort in each other's presence and felt left out.

Jay knew deep within himself lay a strong hidden identity.

He had controlled this overwhelming sense of insecurity, afraid that if he admitted this, everything would be disrupted.

"Varun, you really don't understand?" Jay asked with an unconscious rage in his eyes.

"I don't know what to say. I thought we were way past that."

Shocked at his response, Jay raised an eyebrow, questioning Varun with his firm tone, *"Way past...that?"* and he walked away from the room.

This internal struggle took a toll on Jay's mental state.

He started distancing from Zoya. Both of them went on a silent break in their friendship. In the meantime, Varun felt the guilt of not being able to be the soundboard to Zoya, as he allowed himself to become emotionally invested in Jay's mental struggle, which led Jay to assume a connection that was not meant for him.

Varun was too loyal a friend to Jay and as a business partner, he knew what was at risk. Yet, he allowed Jay's emotions to seep in and could not restrict the growing connection he felt. He didn't want to hurt his best friend's sentiments but got caught up in an unstated commitment.

A few days later over a phone call, *"Zoya, I know I've been really caught up. I don't know how to get out of this. But we can't hurt Jay, he is vulnerable."*

"Vulnerable? And what about me? What and how am I supposed to feel? You know how Jay distanced himself from me. He has been acting weird ever since he got to know about us." Zoya wasn't aware of the emotional complexities that were brewing around her; she couldn't find herself to understand Varun's unacceptable reconnection.

Months passed, and the tension between the three grew; the business got affected. Their connection changed; it got weaker, and they felt more distant from each other. It looked like their friendship had crumbled. Varun held onto silence because he was unsure and felt he had to stay loyal to the times when promises were made.

It was the misplaced loyalty that was the most damaging to Jay and was the only one that could have broken him.

Full circle, he stands in the same hour that had once rejected him. His love confession towards Varun had been rejected years ago. The fact that Varun didn't return his love still today drove him to the brink of madness.

Brushing his fingertips on the compass tattoo, he whispered to himself, *"I wish I could reverse time and erase the moment I wore my heart on my sleeve."*

***

What boundaries have you set for yourself, and how do they reflect your personal growth?

NINTH STITCH

The Bottled Regrets

By Sneha Singh

Aria emerged from the waterlogged airport terminal, her heels dipped a few centimetres in the rainwater. It was the typical Chennai monsoon rain that was gently embracing the tarmac. *"I feel flash blinded from all the explosion of colour.. the vibrant saris.. the chaotic sound of traffic, and ohhh this alluring scent of street food,"* Aria expressed aloud speaking to thin air. *"Suddenly after two years from the blandness of my student life in London School of Business, I have encountered all of this! Ahh! Vande Mataram!"* she continues speaking to thin air.

After years at the prestigious college in London, armed with a degree in business management and a heart brimming with ambition, she had returned to her motherland, India.

Awaiting her with outstretched arms was her father, a sharp-witted industrialist, quite famous among the top entrepreneurs in Chennai and in the whole of South India. Along with him was the chauffeur, who sheltered her under an umbrella as she stepped into the sleek black BMW. *"Such a gorgeous car Appa (dad), Ennadaa idhu! Appaada! (What is this?! Oh my goodness!)"* Aria spoke excitedly, in her London accent.

"That's a gift from your father, my darling daughter! It's a symbol of celebration for your homecoming," her Appa said, blessing her with his palm on her head.

The engine hummed to life. Aria said to her Appa, *"Ahh, I feel the weight of privilege settling on my shoulders like a finely tailored cloak."* They both giggled.

In that moment, as raindrops danced on the car's windshield, she glimpsed the duality of her existence and said, *"Appa, I notice the collision of tradition and modernity, the clash of old-world values and my new-age aspirations. The monsoon feels like it's washing away the cobwebs of my London life, making me feel like I've been reborn on this familiar soil, with all its contradictions. India is the land of opportunities and it has awaited me, so I could write her story, a story of resilience, passion, and the promise of tomorrow."*

And so, as the BMW glided through the wet streets, Aria contemplated her future. The echoes of ancestral wisdom mingled with the pulse of global ambition within her. *"I am no longer just Aria, I am like a bridge between the worlds, I am like a melting pot of cultures and also the embodiment of my father's legacy,"* Aria said to thin air.

And so, with the engine's purr becoming her soundtrack and her real-life background music, she embarked on this homecoming voyage, her heart beating in sync with the rhythm of the monsoon rain.

Aria was active on social media. Her bio said, *"Midnight Hair | Universe's Secrets in My Eyes"*. Her pinned post with a picture of her with the London Eye in the background read - *"I'm the connoisseur of life's finer things like the delicate brushstrokes of a Monet and of course, the artistry of food."*

One evening, as she scrolled through her Instagram feed, a vibrant photo caught her eye. It was a plate of saffron-infused biryani, each grain glistening like a promise. The caption read, *"@SaffronWhispers: Where Flavour Meets Destiny,"* followed by a lot of food-related hashtags, some of which Aria followed and hence landed on this attractive biryani picture.

Curiosity aroused, and Aria clicked on the profile. There, amidst a lot of food shots and kitchen glimpses, she found

Kabir, the chef and owner, behind the culinary magic that spoke through his food pictures. His bio was cryptic, although very intriguing: *"Dreamer. Spice Whisperer. Seeker of Hidden Flavours."* She hit the *'Follow'* button, her heart fluttering like a newly hatched butterfly.

A week later, Aria received a notification: *@kabirwhocooks* had followed her back. She stared at her phone, wondering if the pixels could hold any secrets. She felt encouraged by the anonymity of the digital realm, and she sent him a direct message:

> *Aria: "Hi Kabir! Your saffron biryani looks divine. Any chance you'd share the recipe?"*

Minutes stretched into hours, and just when Aria thought her message had vanished into the ether, a reply appeared:

> *Kabir: "Ah, the saffron biryani, it's the muse of my kitchen. But recipes are like love letters, aren't they? They reveal their magic only when whispered in person. How about a tasting session at 'Saffron Whispers'?"*

Their first meeting was orchestrated by the pixels and emojis. They settled on a date, and Aria arrived at the restaurant, her heart aflutter. There was a neon sign, *'Saffron Whispers'* above her as she stepped inside. Kabir stood there, with his salt-and-pepper beard framing a smile that held more warmth than the early morning sunshine.

The tasting session was a symphony of flavours. Kabir served her the saffron biryani, each spoonful unravelling stories of distant lands and forgotten spices. They talked about life, love, and the alchemy of food. Aria's fingers brushed against his as he handed her a dessert, a rose-scented *Gulab*

Jamun (Rose Berries). Their eyes locked, blushes exchanged, and in that moment, the restaurant faded away, leaving only them, the heiress and the restaurateur.

Back in her apartment, Aria's phone buzzed. It was Kabir:

> *Kabir: "Did the biryani whisper to your soul?"*
>
> *Aria: "Whisper? OMG, it sang an entire opera. But what are all those secrets in your eyes?"*

And so began their digital courtship, texts and emojis kept flowing day in and day out. Late nights turned into early mornings as they exchanged messages:

> *Kabir: "Tonight, the moon is a saffron crescent. Wish you were here."*
>
> *Aria: "I'll bring the stars. And maybe a dash of cardamom."*

Their Instagram stories became a place to share their feelings. They often tagged each other in posts. Kabir shared a picture of a saffron flower with the city skyline in the background. Aria responded with a photo of her balcony garden, where her basil plant looked like it was glowing in the moonlight.

One evening, Kabir messaged her:

> *Kabir: "Rooftop garden, midnight. Bring your favourite spice."*

And so, under a saffron-streaked sky, they met. Kabir held out a small box that had a single vanilla bean. Aria produced a tiny jar of star anise. They laughed, their laughter echoing off the city's walls.

As they sat there, legs dangling over the edge, Kabir whispered, *"Aria, you're my favourite flavour."*

And in that rooftop garden, amidst whispers and spices, they sealed their fate. A love story has started simmering like a slow-cooked curry, fragrant and unforgettable.

Aria smiled and said, *"Your salt-and-pepper beard frames your lips, which quietly share recipes with the wind, holding secrets that may have been passed down for generations."*

Aria and Kabir were an unlikely pairing by societal standards. Although they didn't bother and danced their delicate waltz. She, the heiress to a fortune built on steel and glass, seeking solace beyond her bejewelled cage and he was the culinary alchemist who transformed humble ingredients into magic.

Their conversations flowed like a river. They spoke about saffron threads and the starlit skies, about forbidden spices and forgotten melodies.

The town that was always hungry for gossip wagged its collective tongue. *"What business does she have with a mere restaurateur?"* they murmured, their judgement as sharp as a knife's edge. But the chemistry between Aria and Kabir defied the labels.

In the heart of *'Saffron Whispers'* where neon signs glowed like promises, the two found their place. Their love was like a hidden spice, blending into every dish. Each bite held a memory, and every sip a confession. The heiress and the restaurateur, brought together by flavours and fate, etched their story into the walls of the restaurant.

One moonlit evening, the city revealed its secrets to Kabir and Aria. Their footsteps echoed as they climbed the narrow stairs leading to *'Celestial'*, a hidden rooftop lounge. The air was filled with the scent of jasmine and anticipation. As they stepped outside, the city lights and breeze spread before them like a canvas of dreams.

Kabir held the door open for Aria as she stepped onto the rooftop, her heels clicking on the worn tiles. The city buzzed below them, with the sound of car horns, distant chatter, and the occasional saxophone melody drifting from a nearby jazz club.

Celestial was a hidden gem, known only to a lucky few, both elegant and expensive. The wooden deck, lit by fairy lights, bathed the faces of lovers and dreamers in a soft glow as they admired the luxury around them. At one end was the bar, where the bartender mixed drinks like magic, as if they were made of stardust. Kabir led Aria to a corner table, where a single candle flickered, casting a shadow over their joined hands.

"The champagne has arrived! Look at the crystal glasses, with bubbles rising like forgotten wishes." Aria enjoyed the moment, as Kabir's fingers gently traced patterns on her skin, connecting invisible dots. He spoke of morning dew and cardamom that carried whispers with the breeze.

"Tell me," Aria said, sipping her champagne, tasting the delicate notes of apricot and moonbeams, her eyes reflecting the starlight, *"What's your favourite memory?"*

He smiled, a constellation forming on his lips. *"This,"* he said, gesturing to the rooftop, the city, and the stars. *"This moment. When you and I decided to be each other's secret."*

The BMW was now *'theirs'*, which had become their chariot, more than just a car - it was their vessel of freedom, their escape from the mundane.

Kabir was always the navigator. He knew every twist and turn, every shortcut that led to an undiscovered corner of the city. Aria trusted him implicitly; her fingers would keep tracing the leather upholstery as they sped through moonlit streets.

They discovered hidden alleys where Kabir would just park the BMW, and they'd step out, hand in hand, into a world that seemed to be untouched by time. They'd talk about life, love, and the spaces in between. The BMW waited outside, its headlights casting a protective glow on the two.

And then there were the reckless nights, the ones when they threw caution out to the wind. Kabir would rev the engine, and they'd race through empty streets. It would almost seem like the city lights were blurring into streaks of colour. Aria's laughter would fill the car, and Kabir's eyes would crinkle at the corners.

Their friends were the glitterati who frequently visited Kabir's restaurant. They would often raise their eyebrows. *"You two and that BMW,"* they'd say, sipping champagne, *"It's like a love affair."*

And it was. Aria and Kabir flaunted their love shamelessly. They'd arrive at parties, stepping out of the BMW like celebrities.

But it was more than that. The BMW was their confidant, who would get to silently witness it all. It held their laughter, their tears, and the promises they made under star-studded skies. When Kabir proposed, it was in the backseat, the leather warm against Aria's trembling fingers. She said yes, and the car seemed to purr as it always did, although this time in approval.

Then one night, bathed in moonlight and mischief, Kabir, Aria, and their friends teetered on the edge of recklessness. The BMW, sleek and daring, stood ready, hinting at speed and hidden stories. Too many cocktails had blurred the line between reality and adventure for all of them.

The bunch included actors with brooding gazes, artists with paint-streaked hands, and influencers who wielded hashtags like spells. Their friends, Nisha, Vikram, and Priya, clung to the leather seats. The BMW, usually a symbol of Kabir's success, now became a vessel for their collective madness.

The night was a mix of neon lights and laughter, a wild concoction driven by youth and liquid courage. Aria, with her dark eyes and a heart hungry for adventure, danced on the edge of chaos. Beside her was Kabir, with his salt-and-pepper beard now stained with spilled beer.

Aria's cheeks were flushed from the mix of alcohol and excitement. She swayed as she handed the keys to Rohan, a flamboyant actor with a flair for drama. He eagerly took them, his eyes shining like sequins, and his grin lighting up the moment. *"Let's race!"* he slurred, his voice growing bolder with each word.

As Rohan commandeered Aria's gleaming BMW, the road stretched before them like a ribbon of tar leading nowhere and everywhere. The stars winked conspiratorially, as if they were urging the group to chase the horizon. But the alcohol was blurring their judgement, and they hurtled forward like a comet with no regard for gravity.

"Faster!" Rohan shouted, his fingers gripping the wheel. The BMW surged, its headlights cutting through the darkness like a sharp knife through a cake. Aria clung to the passenger seat. Her heart's rhythm now matching the rhythm of the BMW's. Kabir sat beside her, his fingers tapping an invisible beat on the seats of the car. The wind whipped her hair, and for a moment, she felt invincible. Kabir's eyes held a mix of exhilaration and caution, the same blend that fuelled their love.

The car's engine roared to life, like a wild animal waking up at night. The city streets seemed to stretch out endlessly in front of them as they sped through. Aria's hair flew in the wind as she laughed wildly, her laughter bouncing off the tall buildings. Their BMW felt like a shooting star racing through the city.

Kabir leaned close, his lips brushing Aria's ear. *"We're immortal tonight,"* he whispered. *"Our love, this car, it's all a part of the same constellation."*

She nodded, her pulse racing. *"And Rohan?"*

Kabir chuckled. *"He's our shooting star. Brilliant, unpredictable, and destined to burn out."*

Rohan swerved suddenly, barely avoiding a street vendor's cart. Everyone in the backseat laughed because they were all breaking the curfew and doing something crazy. The car's tyres seemed to touch the road lightly, leaving a trail of sparks behind them.

As they raced towards the finish line, Aria closed her eyes and imagined a ribbon stretching across the city. The wind felt like freedom and rebellion. The car's engine roared with excitement. In that moment, they were more than just lovers and friends; they were legends, writing their own story in the night.

But fate, being that fickle weaver that it usually is, had other plans. A sharp curve appeared on the fourteen-kilometre-long flyover, like a serpent in the night. Rohan's reflexes faltered, and the BMW skidded, tyres screaming in protest. The glitterati bunch, along with the car, flew in the air and like a ball bounced back onto the flyover but this time, ramming into its boundary wall of the flyover. Their time together was now over, like a broken mirror or a crumpled piece of metal.

The crash was loud and sudden, like thunder. The BMW was crushed like paper, its beautiful shape now twisted and broken. Airbags popped up to protect them. The wheel in front of the driver's seat was hanging in the air, touching the broken wall of the bridge. Everyone felt a lot of pain, and Aria's vision was blurry as she tasted blood.

Kabir, with his eyes wide with shock, reached for her. *"Aria!"* he gasped, his voice raw. She tried to speak, but her ribs protested. The others, Nisha, Vikram, and Priya, tried to stumble out. Their laughter was now replaced by cries of pain.

It felt like the night had broken apart along with their time together. The sirens were loud, and the city was quiet. Aria could see the stars through the broken window of the car. They looked far away and didn't seem to care about what had happened. Rohan, who used to love taking risks, now looked shocked and confused. Their car was a broken mess, a reminder of their reckless actions.

"We're alive," Kabir whispered, cradling Aria's bruised hand. His eyes held secrets of the kind that only accidents and near-death experiences reveal. *"Alive, but broken."*

Aria's tears and blood stained her designer dress. Kabir held her, looking sad and worried. They realised they were not invincible anymore. They were just normal people who had made a bad mistake.

The paramedics came quickly, their voices filled with urgency. They used tools to cut away the metal of the car and pulled the people out. They then took the injured glitterati to waiting ambulances. The police and reporters were also there, taking pictures and videos. Aria felt a lot of pain in her ribs as they lifted her onto a stretcher. Kabir followed, walking slowly and looking confused.

Aria's father, a man of influence and connections, was called upon to pull strings. But even his power couldn't untangle this web of consequences. The lobbyist, smelling blood and money, seized the opportunity. He whispered to the media, painting the glitterati as fallen stars.

The headlines screamed: *"Crumpled BMW Seized in Drunk Driving Bust - Glitterati Faces Reality."* Their names were splashed across newspapers, along with photos of the unfortunate accident; their faces were photographed and recorded for identification. Aria's father tried to shield her, but the lenses of judgement were unyielding. The city watched. The same streets that had once witnessed their laughter now bore witness to their downfall. Their accident did not fetch them any sympathy but more dislike because it was a consequence of drunk driving.

The court case was confusing and stressful. They were fined, had to do community service, and lost their driving licences. The car they loved so much was also taken away. In the hospital, Aria and Kabir lay side by side. The X-rays revealed fractures; her wrist and ribs, and his ankle, were all broken. Multiple bruises blossomed like dark flowers. The others, too, were patched up. All of their laughter was now muted.

"We survived," Aria murmured, her gaze on the ceiling. Kabir's hand found hers, their fingers entwined.

Kabir whispered, *"Maybe this accident was fate's way of slowing us down. It was our poor judgement that has led to these unintended consequences and is the true currency of our story."* Aria nodded, her heart bruised but beating. They had danced on the edge, and now they clung to each other, with a fractured love story, stitched with scars.

What regrets do you hold onto? How can releasing them open new possibilities?

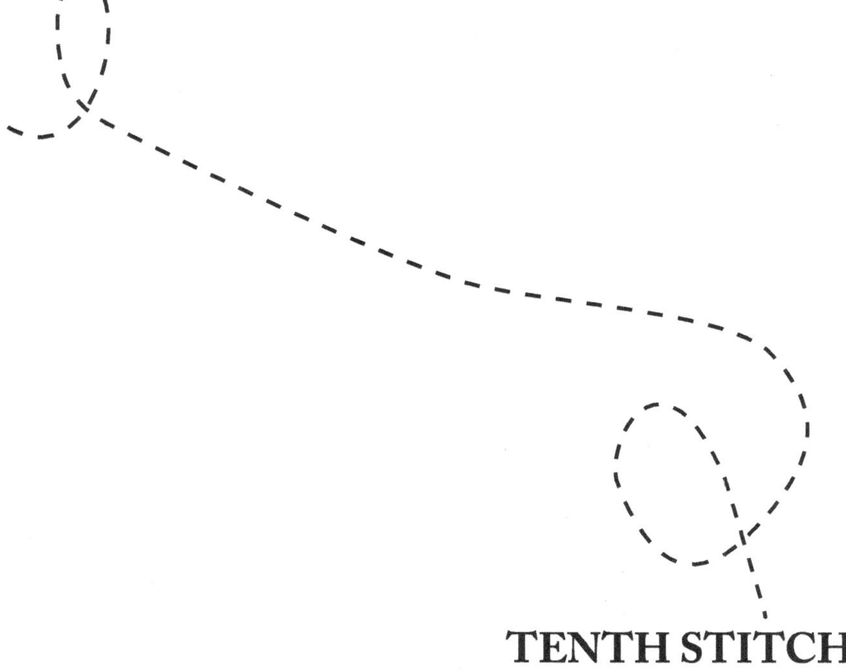

TENTH STITCH

The Chain Of Repeat

By Sarab Kaur

"The lighting in this room is dim," grunted Sid, looking at the tube light, giving a pitying look at his colleague as he entered the subtly typical government office. It was his first day in this office. He walked towards the left where a table was assigned to him and in the corner lay tons of files stacked. *"Look at them, no one can tell apart the floor colour and the files anymore!"* he whispered to himself with disappointment.

He settled his bag and lunchbox on the table and first of all slowly and steadily cleared off the thick layer of dust with his handkerchief, implying they had not been touched in ages. He then separated the files by the dates and cleaned the mites and webs off them.

Next day, at work, as he settled into his dusty table and office chair, he noticed another corner towards the right of his table. He muttered to himself once again, *"Now how can one expect me to work when there are stacks of files towered haphazardly in almost every corner, threatening to spill over at any moment?"* He got up from his wobbly chair, whose one wheel was missing, and it annoyed Sid, as he always felt the inability to sit on it. His co-workers used to find it funny. They assumed it was just a phase and he would get over it soon. One day, one of them said to him, *"Sid ji, this is a government office, that too in Raipur, so what would you even expect? It is impossible to clean up all that while we are loaded with work."* The colleague continued to eat fresh deep-fried hot fritters, making crunchy noises and dropping the crisps on his workbench that had not been cleaned for almost a week and had stains and other food scraps scattered under the keyboard and some papers.

Sid nodded his head and said, *"If you all are too busy doing the work, no problem. I will continue to clean this office for as long as it takes."* As Sid said this, he was taken back to the time when he first realised how messy he used to keep his room and how his mother made him realise the importance of hygiene.

Flashback

"Mom!! Mom!! Why are all these clothes still here and not folded or kept in the wardrobe?" he stormed into his mother's room with a demanding vibe and again questioned her *"Mom!! Why are the clothes piling up on that chair?"* His mother turned around, with a witty expression, and said, *"Why should I always clean up, fold or neaten up things in this house? Is this house solely mine? You live here as well and a helping hand would be wonderful! Anyway, those are your clothes and you need to fold them and keep them where they belong. 'That' is in the closet."* She smirked and continued to browse videos on her phone.

Sid went back into his room to realise the mess he had been making for years and years. The papers on the desk, the cobwebs, the shoes, the socks scattered, and much more. It was the first time that the 14-year-old Sid patiently cleaned up his room and ended up spending 3 hours and more making everything perfect. The clothes were where they belonged, in the closet neatly folded, the shoes cleaned and sanitised, preserved in the shoe boxes.

As years passed, Sid's obsession with cleanliness and order became more prominent.

"Mom! Why is this teacup still kept on the table? And there is a tea stain on the table!" he collects the teacup, washes it off with satisfaction, wipes off the leftover water drops with an absorbent napkin, dries it thoroughly, and keeps it on the shelf with the teacup handle pointing outwards for convenience. He then walks back to the table, sprays the stain remover, and wipes off the whole glass table to have that finished glossy shine.

His mother was impressed with him being responsible for these little things. She was proud of who he was turning out to be and used to gloat about her son's well-mannered behaviour in and around the neighbourhood and family. She thought she was raising a perfect man who did all the chores, excelled in his education, and had a very well-settled, healthy lifestyle. She ignored numerous signs, and he was getting obsessed with cleaning the cluster. His dedication to tidiness interfered with his ability to focus on work, as his anxiousness and irritability grew stronger and stronger.

Over a few weeks, Sid's relationship with his colleagues became strained. He became the subject of gossip and ridicule, which further exacerbated his anxiety. One day, sitting in his office, his boss approached him with dismay. *"Sid, it has just been about 2 months since you joined us here. Your merits and results assured us you will be an asset to this government office, but all I have noticed is that you are more concerned about cleaning up the files and cobwebs here and there. This is not your job and not your place. Please focus on the completion of the project handed over to you and hand it over to me on my desk in time."*

Sid sat there in his wobbly chair, nodded his head, and smiled creepily. As soon as his boss left, Sid started to arrange the pens and papers in the order of their colour, date, and time. He cleaned up the drawers and tried to focus on his work, although the chatty noises around him of his co-workers did not let him concentrate.

He stood up and stormed out of the office building to catch his breath. Standing there, he noticed the building, how its exterior was coated in layers of grime and dust. The vibrant colours of the walls were faded and peeling under the harsh sun. The air inside was too thick with the musty smell of old papers, mildew, and a hint of rot from the scraps of food on other tables. The only way he held onto his sanity was by having a window right behind his desk.

He whispered to himself, *"Look at the ceiling fan, Sid, their blades are covered in dirt and it is rotating so slowly, making this rhythmic creaky sound that echoes in the whole office room. How can the boss expect me to focus on my work in such an ambience!?"* And he quietly typed on his old slow computer.

One night, as he wrote his diary entry, he decided to take a break from his work. He couldn't stand the uncomfortable, messy office on a daily basis. He looked out of the window. The sky was dusky blue, dotted with twinkling stars.

Sid took a deep breath and lay on the bed, closed his eyes but as soon as he closed them, all his brain would automatically dissect *'what's next to clean?'*

"Ah! Why can't I sleep in peace? Why am I always thinking that this is dirty, that is unhealthy, that it is

imperfect? I just can't sleep!" He tosses and turns, only to realise it is morning already. He keeps missing his office without informing them and skips the submission of a very important project.

A few days later, he is notified that he has lost his job.

"Ma, I don't know why I lost this job, I needed a BREAK. All I was doing was cleaning up the space around me so that I could focus on my work. I am not at fault at all! Those people at government offices are just unhygienic and don't care about the ambience. Why is everything so dirty? I can't stop thinking about things being perfect and clean all the time! Do you think I'll ever find someone who's like me, who cares about cleanliness as much as I do? Or will she be totally different? I do not feel satisfied about anything..." He went on and on about all his issues and ended his statements with frustration and anger.

Seeing him so stressed, his mother got worried, although she knew what she had groomed him into. A conflicting personality was emerging. She tried to convince herself that he was normal, but like many parents in their sixties, she turned to Google to research his symptoms. When she couldn't figure out the issue, she eventually called her sister, who lived in Bangalore, for advice.

She discovered that Sid has a condition called OCD.

His mother was hesitant and nervous, yet she spoke.

"I don't know how to say this, but... I think there's something more going on with you. The way you obsess over everything

being clean - it's not normal, Sid. I think you might need help. It could be... an OCD."

Snapping and getting defensive, Sid responded, *"OCD? Are you serious, Ma? You think I have a disorder just because I want things clean? There's nothing wrong with me! You've always taught me to be sharp, crisp and clean!"*

She pleaded, *"Please, just listen! I'm not saying there's anything wrong with you, but this - it's more than just being neat. You're consumed by it! I'm worried about you."*

Sid got furious and was fuming with anger. He raised his voice, *"Worried? You're making it sound like I'm mad! I'm fine, okay? I just care about things being right, being perfect. What's wrong with that?"*

Her voice shakes as she is almost in tears, *"It's not just about being perfect! You're torturing yourself. You can't relax, you can't work on anything because all you see is dirt, mess. I can see it in your eyes. It's eating you alive! Please, just talk to someone!"*

This time Sid's rage is out of control. He clenches his fists, stands up, and yells, *"No! I'm not crazy, Ma! I don't need a doctor or a therapist to tell me how to live my life! You just don't get it!"*

His mother's eyes start streaming with tears, yet she tries to stay calm. *"I do get it! I see how much this is controlling you, and it's breaking my heart. I just want to help you. Why won't you let me?"*

Sid yells right back at her, *"Because there's nothing to help! I'm not broken! I don't need fixing! You're the one who doesn't understand me!"*

He storms out, slamming the door, claiming it to his mother for one last time. ***"There's nothing wrong with me!"***

The tension between his denial and her concern ended up in a painful conversation.

A few weeks later:

Girl, muttering softly to herself, searching through the shelves, *"Hmm, where did that mango pickle go? I swear I just saw it here..."* Sid heard her murmur and, smiling, held out a jar, giving it to her. *"Looking for this?"* She was startled but amused. *"Oh! Yes, that's the one. Thank you!"*

She took the jar from his hand; her eyes met his for a brief second. There was something about her, a quiet curiosity, a softness that made Sid's heart skip. She was just another shopper, yet something pulled him in.

Sid nervously tried to keep the conversation going. *"You've got a good taste. Mango pickle is the best,"* she laughed and said with a playful smile, *"Yeah, I guess I'm a sucker for anything tangy."* From that moment, something clicked. They didn't know each other, but it felt like they did.

Over the next few weeks, what started as casual encounters in the store turned into something more. Sid found himself drawn to Geeta. Their conversations grew longer, more personal, until one day, they were sitting in a cafe, talking about life as if they had known each other for years.

"You know, Sid... there's something about you. You always seem so... put together. Like you've got everything in control." Sid's heart skipped a beat. He wasn't as put together as she thought. His mind was always racing - counting, cleaning, organising. The compulsion to control everything consumed him. He had been hiding it from her, terrified that she would see him differently. But now, with her eyes searching for him, it felt like the moment had come.

Hesitantly, looking down, Sid starts, *"I need to tell you something. I'm not as... in control as you think."*

"Ahh... you're just saying this for the heck of it, aren't you?!" Geeta noticed his serious face and then looked at him in confusion, asking, *"Okay, Mr. Serious! What do you mean?"*

He didn't want to claim it but somewhere he knew it, he nervously said, *"I... I have OCD. I've tried to hide it, but it's always there. The thoughts, the need to make everything perfect - it never stops."*

For a moment, there was pin-drop silence between them. Sid feared what might come next was going to be rejection or disgust. But instead, she placed her hand gently on his hand and calmly said, *"Sid, you don't have to be perfect with me. I like you for who you are, not for how clean your apartment is."*

Sid surprisingly asked, *"How do you understand me and my issues so flawlessly, whereas the world around me is always pointing fingers at me, blaming me for being compulsive? Where have you been all my life?"* He held her hand with compassion.

"Sid, I haven't been quite honest with you. Actually, hmm, actually I am a therapist by profession, and I was hired by your mother to help you with your OCD because you wouldn't see a professional."

Sid was stunned by her response, which quickly led him to ask, *"So you mean I am your patient and nothing else? So, whatever that is going on between us is all because you felt sympathetic or obligated towards me and were treating me like your patient?"*

"No... no... Sid. I am in love with you and it has absolutely nothing to do with being a therapist to you!" she explained and tried to assure him that her love for him was genuine. But Sid was heartbroken and furious to know that the person whom he fell in love with was just a professional therapist.

"But why hide it from me?" yelled Sid.

"Sid, I wanted to tell you, but I was waiting for the right time. I didn't want our relationship to be defined by my profession." Geeta continued to explain. *"I was afraid you might see me differently, that you'd treat me like I'm analysing you all the time. I just wanted us to be us, not therapists and patients."*

Sid was disappointed, and the bond between them felt forged. He replied with a heartbroken, cracking voice, *"I feel betrayed and humiliated not just by you but by my mother as well. She hired you!! You kept such a big part of yourself from me."*

"I understand how you feel, but please believe me, it was never about deceit. I love you, Sid, and I wanted us to build our relationship on our own terms, not based on my profession."

"I don't know if I can trust you anymore, Geeta. This changes everything."

"Please, Sid, don't let this come between us. I love you with all my heart, and I'll do anything to make things right."

The argument escalated. Emotions were running high as both Sid and Geeta struggled to find common ground amidst feelings of betrayal and hurt. The couple agreed to talk things through and agreed to focus on their future together. Geeta promised her profession wouldn't come between them. She became his constant support. Sid's mother was secretly relieved to see her son becoming normal. With Geeta's efforts and techniques, Sid's daily rituals morphed. What was once a chain of repeat slowly faded away. Geeta handled their conversations to topics that diverted Sid's attention away from his compulsions, allowing him to engage in the ERP (Exposure and Response Prevention) exercises without realising it. During these exercises, Geeta came to understand that Sid's struggles stemmed from a deep-rooted childhood trauma. Another truth emerged - one that was both devastating and revealing. Sid's subconscious mind had been imprinted with the weight of his home's uncleanliness by his mother. The household conditions had been unhygienic, which he assumed contributed to his father's health struggles, followed by the death that occurred years ago.

As Sid dug through his memories, he realised he had been blaming himself for his dad's health issues because of their messy house. But then, while conversing about it with Geeta, he realised something unusual. Sid immediately left for his home, and as soon as he entered the house, he rushed towards his mother and sat her down in their living room.

He started, *"Mom, something really hit me hard about dad."*

His mom's eyes widened with curiosity as she listened intently. *"I've been carrying this guilt, blaming myself for dad's health problems because of our messy house. But then, even before things got messy, dad was already dealing with health issues, right?"*

His mom's expression softened on her face. *"Yes, beta, that's what I've been trying to tell you,"* she said nervously. *"Your dad's health was about so much more than just cleanliness - it was a mix of factors, like genetics and lifestyle."*

His mother hesitated, her face pale as she seemed to be wrestling with her words. Sid asked his mother, *"What is it? Why are you sweating? Is there something more I need to know about, Ma?"* Sid leaned in, looking into his mother's eyes.

She closed her eyes for a moment, gathered the strength to reveal the truth she had buried for years. Softly and barely able to meet his eyes, she mumbled, *"Sid, your father didn't die... he left us."*

Sid's world stopped. His breath caught in his throat as the ground seemed to shift beneath him. *"What? No... no, that's not possible. You told me - Mom, you said he died from a health issue! You* ***told*** *me!"*

She replied with a cracking voice, *"I know, beta. I know. I lied to protect you. I thought if you believed he died, you wouldn't have to carry the pain of him abandoning us... abandoning* ***you****."*

Sid's hands clenched into fists, his mind spinning. *"Abandoned us? Why would he - what happened?"*

His mother, her face twisted with guilt, finally met his gaze. *"It wasn't just his health, Sid. Your father... he couldn't handle it anymore. The mess, the clutter. He couldn't stand living in the chaos, but I couldn't control it. You were too young, and I barely had any support. It became a daily drama between us, and our fights and arguments grew with each passing day. And one day he... he left. He said he couldn't stay with us, he couldn't stay in an unclean house any longer."*

Sid's heart was pounding. Everything he had believed, every shred of guilt he had carried for his father's so-called death, shattered in an instant.

Fuming with anger, he asked, *"So he just... walked away? Because things weren't* ***clean****? And you let me believe he was dead?"*

His mother nodded, sobbing quietly. *"I didn't know how to explain it to you, Sid. You were just a boy. I thought if I told you the truth, it would destroy you. So I told you he passed away. I thought it would be easier for you to live with that."*

Sid screaming in rage, *"Easier?! You let me live with guilt for years - thinking I caused his death because I didn't do enough to keep things clean! And all this time, he's out there, alive?!"*

His mother sobbed harder, *"Sid, your father had OCD too, and it destroyed our marriage. I thought a messy person like me could never break you, so I raised you to be meticulous, to maintain control - hoping that would keep you safe. But then I saw it... you have OCD too. And I couldn't bear it. I couldn't lose you the way I lost him to this madness. I already watched this disease consume your father and tear our family apart. But you... not you. I had to do whatever it took, no matter the cost, to protect you from the same fate."*

The room spun as the reality of it all hit him - his father hadn't died. He had *'left'*.

Sid stood frozen as his mother's words hit him like a tidal wave. His heart pounded, a mixture of anger, shock, and deep sadness swirling inside him.

"You... you knew?" he finally whispered, his voice trembling with disbelief.

"You saw this happening, and instead of helping me, you... pushed me? You thought you could control it by making me

more like him? Do you know how suffocating it's been, feeling like I was never good enough? Like everything had to be perfect?"

His eyes filled with tears, but there was anger in them, too. *"You were so afraid of losing me that you never even let me be me. And now, all this time... I thought I was fighting my own demons, but I was just living in his shadow.*

Your fear, Mom, it didn't save me. It trapped me."

What patterns in your life do you find yourself repeating, and how can you break free?

ELEVENTH STITCH

The Rehoming Dilemma

By Sneha Singh

Sudevi looked at her husband with stern eyes and said, *"Mr Vallabh Dhar, please, it's a request, the boys are forever glued to their screens. You know I was at the staff room today when I heard my colleagues discussing how screen addiction can lead to problems with social and emotional competence. I have read that it also affects brain development and consequently lowers academic achievement, leading to lower school functioning, and poor maths and language achievement,"* while she was still continuing to speak, Vallabh smiled and said, *"Oh my God women! I don't know what to say, Sudevi ji. You are telling me that not getting a pet for our boys is going to hamper their personality so much?!"* saying so, Vallabh had a hearty laugh and walked across the huge hallway. As his shadow crossed through the window behind him, Mrs. Dhar stared straight through it. In her line of vision, she could see the sun setting into the horizon far away behind the waves of the ocean.

Sudevi, with her husband Vallabh and their sons Adidev and Avyukt, had just moved into their enormous mansion-like police quarter bungalow a little away from the city of Goa. Adidev was ten years old, and Avyukt was just seven. It was truly concerning for Sudevi that the boys had no one to mingle with. It had been about four months since they had moved here, and with her recent joining at the college and the ample house help they had, the boys had nothing much to do except for looking at their screens all day.

Sudevi walked behind her husband and kept speaking without stopping, *"They are all the time watching so much nonsense and then playing video games, haven't you seen that we had to get Avyukt glasses. At such a young age Vallabh! I've been requesting you ever since we got here first."*

"Okay, okay, fine Sudevi ji, we will go tomorrow. Let's tell the boys now! Avyukt Adidev come here beta, we have some fun things to disclose to you boys," Vallabh roared as his voice pierced through the huge rooms of the bungalow. Sudevi smiled and adored the conversation between the father and his sons.

As the Dhar family entered the pet store, they saw a bright light pouring through the large windows, throwing a soft glow on the rows of cages and aquariums. Shelves were lined with colourful bags of food, toys, and leashes. Adidev and Avyukt were overjoyed with all of this as they held hands and tugged their parents forward.

"Mom, Dad, look! There are so many dogs!" Adidev pointed excitedly towards the kennel area. His eyes sparkled with excitement as his younger brother bounced beside him, barely able to contain his own energy.

"I want a big dog!" Avyukt chimed in, his voice almost a squeal. *"One we can play with and run around in the yard with!"*

Sudevi smiled softly, glancing at Vallabh. *"Let's take our time and see which one feels right, okay? Remember, a pet is part of the family,"* Sudevi explained to the boys.

The boys nodded in unison, though their eager feet were already pulling their parents towards the section where the dogs were. Rows of cages held puppies and older dogs, some wagging their tails eagerly, others watching quietly with curious eyes.

"Look at this one!" Adidev's voice was high with excitement as he knelt in front of a large kennel. Inside was a

young Pitbull with light grey fur and white markings. He sat quietly, watching the boys with gentle eyes. His tail thumped once, twice against the floor as Adidev made eye contact. *"He's so calm. Can we meet him?"*

Avyukt crouched beside his brother, his small hand reaching through the bars cautiously. The Pitbull leaned forward, sniffing at his fingers and then licking them. *"He likes me!"* Avyukt giggled, his eyes wide with joy. *"Mom, Dad, look!"*

Vallabh smiled and signalled for one of the store workers, who approached with a friendly smile and said, *"You guys want to meet him outside the cage?"*

"Yes, please!" Adidev stood up quickly, brushing his hands on his jeans, his heart thudding with anticipation. Avyukt hopped up and down excitedly, unable to stand still.

The store worker opened the cage, and the Pitbull stepped out cautiously, its head low, but tail wagging. The boys instantly dropped to their knees to greet him. The dog sniffed them both before licking Adidev's face, making him giggle uncontrollably.

"He's perfect!" Adidev declared, scratching the dog behind his ears. *"Can we take him home, Mom? Please?"*

Sudevi knelt beside them, rubbing the dog's back as she studied the calm, friendly animal. *"He does seem sweet, doesn't he?"* She looked over at Vallabh, who chuckled.

"Well, boys, having a pet dog is a big responsibility. You'll have to take care of him, feed him, walk him... mmm also clean his poop until he's fully trained."

"We will!" the boys interrupted, their voices filled with determination. *"I'll do everything, I promise!"* each of them kept saying.

"I'll help too!" Vallabh added, hugging the dog's neck as it sat down beside them, clearly content with the attention.

The Pitbull leaned into Adidev's hug, his tail thumping on the floor. The worker smiled. *"He's a good one. Gentle, but strong. He'll be a noble companion,"* he affirmed.

After a few minutes of talking and watching the boys bond with the dog, Sudevi stood up. *"Alright. Let's take him home."*

The boys erupted in cheers, Avyukt pumping his fist in the air while Adidev practically danced on the spot he was standing on.

As they filled out the adoption paperwork, Adidev whispered to Avyukt, *"What should we name him?"*

Avyukt, his face serious as he thought, said, *"How about Zeus?"*

Adidev grinned. *"Zeus!! Yeah, that's perfect."*

On the drive home, Zeus sat calmly between the boys in the backseat, his head resting on Adidev's lap, while Avyukt kept stroking his soft fur. The two boys couldn't stop smiling.

"I can't believe we have a dog," Adidev said quietly, his voice filled with wonder. *"I've wanted one for so long."*

"Me too!" Avyukt whispered, resting his head on Zeus's back. *"We're gonna be best friends forever."*

Sudevi and Vallabh exchanged a look in the front seat, smiling at the sight of their boys so happy and content with their new companion.

Six happy months with Zeus had passed. Zeus, once the gentle little puppy the boys had adored, had grown into a powerful dog. His muscular frame moved with a tense energy, always ready to pounce. The yard, which used to be a place of carefree play for the boys, had become a place of caution.

Adidev and Avyukt were playing with Zeus, but the laughter had a nervous edge to it. Avyukt, the younger of the two, winced as Zeus barrelled past him, brushing against his arm with his thick body.

"Avyukt, he's getting too rough," Adidev said, rubbing a fresh bruise forming on his forearm. His voice was small, conflicted between his love for Zeus and the growing fear that the dog was becoming too much.

"It's okay, Avyukt, he's just playing..." Adidev reassured his brother, but even he couldn't shake the nervous look in his eyes. He glanced at Zeus, who was pacing now, his eyes fixed on the soccer ball with an intensity that made Adidev uneasy. *"Right, boy?"*

Zeus barked sharply, startling both of them.

Inside the house, Sudevi stood at the kitchen sink, watching through the window with worry inevitably etched across her face. She couldn't help but notice the boys' discomfort, the way they hesitated now before petting Zeus, always watching for a sudden movement.

"Vallabh, this can't go on," she said, her voice strained as she turned to her husband, who was sitting at the dining table, flipping through the bills. *"The boys are covered in bruises. Meena is reluctant to stay along with the boys throughout the*

day; she's so afraid to come near him, and I don't know how much longer we can pretend this isn't a problem."

Vallabh sighed heavily, rubbing his temples. *"He's just high-energy, Sudevi ji. Pit bulls are muscular dogs. We knew that when we got him."*

"But he's not just strong anymore, Vallabh!" Sudevi shot back, her voice raising slightly. *"He's scaring them. They're too young for this kind of responsibility. And we haven't even started talking about what happened with my colleague Sheela when I invited her over along with me the other day."*

Vallabh frowned. *"That was an accident. He didn't mean to tear her dress; he was just being playful."*

"Being playful shouldn't involve lunging at guests and ripping their clothes," Sudevi said, her frustration mounting. *"Do you really think she'll come over again after that? She was terrified and embarrassed at the same time."*

Vallabh didn't have an answer for that, so he stood up and walked to the window, watching the boys cautiously pass the soccer ball while keeping one eye on Zeus. The dog's behaviour was becoming more erratic, more unpredictable, and it was no longer something he could dismiss as just *'puppy energy'*.

Just then, the front door creaked open, and Meena, their housekeeper, stepped inside, her face pale. She looked around cautiously, clearly on edge.

"Didi..." Meena began, her voice trembling slightly, *"I can't stay anymore. Zeus... he tried to bite me again when I was cleaning the hall this morning."*

Sudevi's heart sank. *"Meena, I'm so sorry. He's just... He's been more difficult to control lately, but we're working on it."*

"I know, Didi, but I'm afraid. I have children of my own. I can't take the risk anymore." Meena's eyes darted nervously to the yard where Zeus was pacing, his tail stiff, his eyes locked on the boys. *"I'm sorry, but I have to go."*

Without another word, Meena quickly gathered her things and hurried out of the house, leaving Sudevi standing there feeling helpless.

"See? Even she fears him." Sudevi said quietly, turning to Vallabh, her voice heavy with worry.

Vallabh sighed again, rubbing the back of his neck. *"I'll talk to the trainer again. Maybe we need more sessions, or maybe..."*

"Maybe what?" Sudevi asked, her tone soft but urgent. *"Vallabh, this isn't just about training anymore. He's a Pitbull, and people are going to judge him for his breed. He's getting bigger, stronger and more aggressive. What if something worse happens?"*

As they spoke, a sudden loud yelp came from outside. Both parents rushed to the back door to find Avyukt sitting on the ground, tears streaming down his face, clutching his arm where Zeus had bitten him - not hard, but enough to leave a deep red mark and a little blood. Adidev was trying to hold Zeus back, but the dog was growling, pulling against his hold, eyes wild with energy.

"Avyukt! Are you okay?" Sudevi ran to her younger son, kneeling beside him.

"It hurts, Mom," Avyukt whimpered, his voice shaking with a mixture of fear and confusion. *"He didn't mean it, I know he didn't, but..."*

"But he did it." Adidev finished for him, his voice full of uncertainty. He looked at Zeus, the dog he loved so much, and for the first time, he felt a knot of fear tighten in his chest. "He's not the same, Mom. I don't know what's happening to him."

Vallabh stepped forward, gripping Zeus's collar firmly. *"Zeus, down!"* he ordered, but the dog resisted, still growling low in his throat.

Sudevi stood up, pulling Avyukt into her arms as tears welled in her eyes. *"Vallabh, we can't keep doing this. What if next time he bites harder? What if it's not one of the boys, but someone else? We have to think about this seriously."*

Adidev, still standing next to Zeus, whispered, *"But I love him, Mom. We can't just get rid of him. He's our pet."*

Sudevi's heart broke at the sound of her son's voice, but she exchanged a pained look with Vallabh, who finally nodded, his face grim.

"We'll talk about it, Adidev." Vallabh said softly, though he already knew the decision was looming in their future. *"But we need to do what's safest for everyone, okay?"*

The weight of the words hung heavily in the air as Adidev and Avyukt stared at Zeus, their beloved pet, who was now becoming a danger to the home they had once shared so happily.

It was a few weeks later on a quiet afternoon at home. Adidev and Avyukt were in the living room, after school, playing with their video game while Zeus lounged nearby, his colossal frame taking up most of the couch. The boys had become more cautious around him lately, but today Adidev felt a little more at ease.

"Pass me the car, Avyukt," Adidev said, stretching his arm towards his younger brother who was rolling a toy car on the floor.

Avyukt handed it over, glancing at Zeus. The dog's eyes flicked between the boys, alert but calm for the moment.

"Zeus seems better today," Adidev remarked, trying to reassure both himself and Avyukt. *"Maybe he's just been bored lately. Mom said he needs more exercise."*

"Yeah..." Avyukt mumbled, though his gaze stayed wary, still remembering the bite weeks ago and, needless to say, the scratches.

But just as Adidev leaned forward to grab the car, Zeus jolted up, his ears back, and a low growl rumbled in his throat. In an instant, he leapt at Adidev, jaws snapping around the boy's face before anyone could react.

A scream tore through the room.

Adidev fell backwards, clutching his face, blood pouring from between his fingers. *"Avyukt! Help me!"* His voice was muffled, filled with pain and terror. Zeus stood over him, his growl now replaced with an eerie silence, as if he was confused by his own actions.

Avyukt was frozen, wide-eyed, watching in horror as his brother lay on the floor, a chunk of his cheek hanging from his face, blood spilling onto the carpet.

"A-Adidev..." Avyukt stammered, his whole body trembling. He didn't know what to do, his mind blank with fear. His older brother's cries echoed in his ears, but all he could see was the blood, so much blood.

"A-Avyukt, call... call Mom!" Adidev's words were broken by sobs of agony as he tried to press his hand against the wound, feeling the sting and the warmth of the blood. *"I... I can't..."*

Avyukt finally snapped out of his paralysis and stumbled towards the phone, his hands shaking so hard he almost dropped it. His small fingers fumbled as he dialled their mother's number.

Sudevi was in the middle of a lecture, walking between rows of students with her lesson plan in hand. Her phone, set to vibrate in her bag, buzzed for a moment, but she didn't notice.

The buzzing continued until it stopped briefly, only to start again. Finally, one of her students raised their hand.

"Ma'am, I think your phone has been vibrating." the student pointed out.

Sudevi's brow furrowed, with a slight pang of worry surfacing. She hurried towards her bag and checked the screen - *'Home Calling'* flashed on her phone. The notification bar showing missed calls.

Her heart skipped a beat. Why was *'Home'* calling right after school hours?

She quickly excused herself from the classroom and stepped out into the hallway, answering the call. *"Hello, beta? Is everything okay?"*

But all she heard on the other end was Avyukt's choked sobbing.

"Mom... Mom, it's Adidev!" Avyukt's voice was a frantic whisper, words tumbling out in a panic. *"Zeus... Zeus bit him! There's so much blood... he's hurt badly, Mom! He's bleeding... so much..."*

Sudevi's world froze. Her breath caught in her throat as she pressed the phone harder against her ear, hoping she had heard it wrong. *"What? Avyukt, what are you talking about? Where's Adidev? What happened!"*

"He's on the floor!" Avyukt cried, his voice breaking. *"His face, Mom... Zeus bit his face! There's blood everywhere... I don't know what to do! He's crying and... and there's so much blood!"*

Sudevi's heart pounded so hard she thought it might burst. Her vision blurred for a moment as panic clawed at her chest. *"Oh, my God..." she whispered. "Avyukt, listen to me, beta. You have to stay calm, okay? Is Zeus around?"*

Avyukt glanced at the dog, who was pacing back and forth, whimpering now, confused by the chaos. *"He's not biting anymore, but... Adidev... Mom, you need to come home! Please! Come home NOW!"*

"I'm coming, baby, I'm coming!" Sudevi said, her voice trembling as she rushed toward her car, her hands fumbling for her keys. *"I'm on my way and I'm calling an ambulance, right now, Avyukt! When they come, tell them Adidev is hurt, and we need immediate help. Do you hear me?"*

Avyukt sniffled, his little voice shaking. *"O-okay. I'll tell them. Please hurry, Mom!"*

Sudevi's hands were shaking so violently that she could barely unlock the car door. The image of Adidev lying there, bleeding, filled her mind, and she fought to stay focused. Tears welled in her eyes, but she wiped them away furiously. There wasn't time for panic.

Avyukt, with trembling hands, waited for the ambulance to arrive. He saw Meena Didi rushing towards the house. Sudevi had called her for help since she lived a few metres away from their bungalow. With his choked voice struggling to form the words, he explained what had happened to Meena. Meanwhile, Adidev lay on the floor, groaning in pain, blood still pouring from the wound on his cheek.

"Avyukt... Meena Didiii," Adidev mumbled weakly, his eyes half-closed. *"I'm scared..."*

"I know, Adidev... I know... I'm scared too." Avyukt said, crawling over to his brother and kneeling beside him, tears streaming down his face. Meena reached out, taking Adidev's hand, squeezing it tightly. *"Mom's coming beta. She's coming, okay? The ambulance is also coming."* she reassured Adidev.

The minutes felt like hours, and the sound of sirens finally wailed in the distance. Avyukt and Meena held Adidev's hand, shaking with fear but trying to comfort him as best they could.

"I'm sorry, Adidev," Avyukt whispered, guilt eating at him for not being able to do more. *"I'm so sorry..."*

Adidev didn't respond. His eyes were glassy, his breathing shallow, and the pain was starting to overwhelm him. Blood soaked the carpet beneath his face.

When Sudevi finally arrived home, her car screeched to a halt in the driveway. She didn't even turn off the engine before she threw open the door and rushed into the house. The scene before her was like something out of a nightmare. Adidev, her precious boy, lay on the floor, his face a bloody mess, Avyukt crouched beside him, his cheeks streaked with tears.

"Adidev!" Sudevi screamed, dropping to her knees next to him, her hands hovering, afraid to touch his face. *"Oh my God, Adidev... No, no, no..."*

Adidev's eyes flickered open at the sound of Sudevi's voice, but he was too weak to respond.

"Where's the ambulance?!" Sudevi cried, looking around in a frenzy, her heart shattering with every second that passed.

"It might be coming, Didi..." Meena whispered. *"I called them... they said they will be here in 10 minutes."* Sudevi exclaimed.

Sudevi wrapped her arms around both of her boys, her body trembling with fear and guilt. *"It's okay, baby, it's okay. I'm here now. I'm so sorry, I'm so, so sorry..."*

As the wail of the ambulance drew closer, Sudevi clung to Adidev, praying for the nightmare to end.

In the living room, a few days after the incident, the air in the house felt heavy, suffocating, and with an unspoken tension. Adidev had just come home from the hospital, his cheek bandaged, stitches running across his face. The swelling had gone down, but the pain, both physical and emotional, was lingering.

Sudevi sat on the couch, wringing her hands, her eyes fixed on the ground. Across from her, Vallabh stood by the window, his face set in a tight frown as he looked outside, avoiding eye contact. Zeus sat in the corner, unaware of the turmoil, occasionally lifting his head to watch the family with his usual alertness.

The boys were on the floor, Adidev sitting close to Avyukt, his face pale but determined. There was a palpable sense of dread in the air. Everyone knew why they were gathered here. No one wanted to start the conversation.

Sudevi took a deep breath, her heart racing. Her voice came out soft, almost a whisper. *"We need to talk... about Zeus."*

Adidev's head shot up, his wide eyes locking with his mother's. Avyukt, sitting beside him, instinctively grabbed his brother's arm, sensing the tension.

"What do you mean, Mom?" Adidev asked, though deep down, he already knew. His voice trembled slightly, and he shifted uncomfortably. *"He didn't mean to hurt me. It wasn't his fault."*

Avyukt chimed in, his voice small and pleading. *"He's a good dog, Mom. He didn't know... He didn't mean it."*

Sudevi's chest tightened at their words, a lump forming in her throat. She glanced at Vallabh, who gave her a solemn nod, silently telling her to continue. She swallowed hard and turned back to her sons, her eyes misting with tears.

"I know you love Zeus..." she began, her voice choking with emotion. *"I love him too. But after what happened with Adidev... we have to face the truth. He's become too dangerous to keep."*

Adidev shook his head, his face paling even more. *"No, Mom, no. He didn't mean it! It was an accident! I... I shouldn't have leaned in so close. It's my fault, not his."*

Sudevi's heart broke at the sight of Adidev defending the dog that had nearly disfigured him. Tears brimmed in her eyes, but she forced herself to stay strong. *"Sweetheart, it wasn't your fault. You're just a kid. You did nothing wrong, okay? Zeus is... he's unpredictable now. What if he hurts you again? What if it's worse next time?"*

"He won't! He won't!" Adidev insisted, his voice cracking. *"Please, Mom, don't make us get rid of him. He's my best friend."*

Avyukt's lip quivered, and he turned to Vallabh. *"Dad, tell her we don't have to. We can train him more. We can keep him away from guests or... or get a big fence in the yard. We'll be careful, I promise!"*

Vallabh's face contorted with grief as he crouched down to their level, taking both boys' hands in his. His voice was calm but firm. *"Boys, we've tried. We've done everything we can to help Zeus, but this... this isn't safe anymore. We have to think about what's best for our family."*

Adidev's face crumpled, tears spilling over as he clutched at his bandaged cheek, the pain still fresh in his mind but his love for Zeus fighting against his fear. *"But he's family, Dad," Adidev whispered, his voice barely audible. "You can't just give him away... He's family..."*

Avyukt, sobbing now, crawled over to Zeus, wrapping his small arms around the dog's neck. *"Zeus doesn't want to go! He loves us! You can't send him away!"* he cried, burying his face in Zeus's fur. Zeus licked Avyukt's face, unaware of the heartache he was causing, his tail wagging softly.

Sudevi wiped her eyes, her heart splitting in two. She knelt down next to Adidev, pulling him into her arms as he sobbed against her chest. Her voice cracked as she spoke. *"I'm so sorry, Adidev. I'm so, so sorry. I'm sorry, beta Avyukt, I know how much this hurts you. I wish things were different, but I can't let this happen again. I can't risk losing you... or Avyukt."*

Adidev's sobs grew louder, his fingers clutching at his mother's saree. *"Please don't take him, Mom. Please don't..."*

Sudevi held him tighter, her own tears now flowing freely. She felt like the worst mother in the world, but she knew she was doing what she had to - what any parent would. She looked over at Vallabh, her eyes begging for strength, but she could see he was barely holding it together too.

Vallabh cleared his throat, his voice thick with emotion. *"It's not easy for us either, boys. We love Zeus, we really do. But your safety has to come first."*

Avyukt, still hugging Zeus, screamed through his tears. *"No! It's not fair! I don't want him to go! He's my brother!"*

Zeus, sensing the tension, let out a soft whine, nuzzling Avyukt's face. Sudevi's heart twisted painfully, watching her young son clutch the dog as if his world would shatter if he let go.

"I know, Avyukt," she whispered, kneeling beside him now, gently placing a hand on his back. *"I know how much you love him. And this isn't fair. It's the hardest thing we've ever had to do. But... we need to find him a place where he won't hurt anyone. A place where he can be safe, and you can be safe too."*

Avyukt shook his head violently. *"But we're his family! He came to us as a little baby."*

Sudevi's voice broke as she whispered, *"I know, bacha (child). I know."*

Adidev pulled away from Sudevi, wiping his face, his eyes red and swollen. He looked at Zeus, then back at his parents, his body shaking with sobs. *"Will we ever see him again?"* he asked, his voice weak, filled with a quiet, heartbreaking acceptance that this was the end.

Vallabh's face crumpled, and he crouched next to Adidev. *"We'll make sure he goes to a good home, okay? Someone who can take care of him the way he needs. But it's going to be hard... and I don't think it's a good idea to see him again."*

Adidev bit his lip, a fresh wave of tears spilling down his cheeks. He didn't say anything, just nodded, knowing deep down that this was a goodbye.

Zeus, sensing the sadness in the room, let out a small bark, his head tilted in confusion. He trotted over to Adidev, nuzzling his hand, his tail wagging as if nothing had changed. But everything had.

As Adidev stroked Zeus's head, his touch gentle and full of sorrow, he whispered, *"I'll miss you, Zeus. I'll miss you so much."*

Sudevi stood back, her hands trembling as she watched her boys say their silent goodbyes. She turned to Vallabh, her voice a broken whisper. *"How are we supposed to live with this?"*

Vallabh placed a hand on her shoulder, his own face streaked with tears. *"We have to do it because we love them. Because we have to keep them safe, Sudevi ji."*

Sudevi nodded, but the weight of their decision pressed down on her, and she knew this moment would leave a scar on all of them, a scar that would never fully heal.

Have you ever had to choose between the lesser of the two evils? How did you heal from it?

TWELFTH STITCH

The Sync of Freedom

By Sarab Kaur

Amar woke to the soft hum of his PIXI smartwatch vibrating against his wrist. Its gentle voice followed, calm yet commanding.

"Good morning, Amar. Time to wake up for your morning routine."

He blinked groggily at the ceiling, the blue glow of his smart blinds opening. The city outside was already humming with the low buzz of a million devices, all whirring and clicking in perfect sync. PIXI showed him his schedule: hydration reminder, 10-minute meditation, then a quick ECG check before breakfast.

Routine. All perfectly timed. PIXI kept him in line, kept him healthy, kept him safe.

Amar was all of twenty-six, fit, and probably healthier than most people he knew. Not that he'd ever really checked himself - PIXI did that for him. Blood oxygen, heart rate, sleep cycle, steps, calories. Everything he did, everything he felt, was meticulously monitored and analysed by his gadgets. It wasn't just a lifestyle; it was a way of life.

"Your ECG is scheduled in five minutes," PIXI chimed, its familiar cool tone breaking through Amar's grogginess. He yawned and stretched, muscles already anticipating the analysis. *"Of course."* he muttered to himself, getting out of bed and reaching for his smart glasses. A flash of the city skyline appeared before his eyes, a towering maze of shimmering glass and buzzing neon. Streets below were filled with people rushing about, heads down, eyes glued to screens, smart rings glowing on their fingers.

He showered, ate his scientifically balanced breakfast, and finally sat down for his ECG scan. PIXI had been reminding him for days to do it, and there was no avoiding it now.

The little gadget on his wrist began to scan his vitals. Amar felt fine—great, actually. But as the scan finished, PIXI's tone shifted, just slightly. He couldn't be sure, but it sounded almost… concerned.

"Something's not right," PIXI said softly.

Amar's heart skipped. *"What do you mean?"*

"Your heart rate is irregular. Possible arrhythmia detected. You should rest and consider visiting a clinic."

Amar stared at the screen. He felt fine. Better than fine, actually. No dizziness, no pain, no shortness of breath. But PIXI didn't lie. It couldn't. His stomach tightened. If the smartwatch said something was wrong, it had to be true.

"Rest," PIXI repeated, a little more insistent this time.

His mind raced. He felt anxious, his pulse quickening - was that the arrhythmia? Or was he just overthinking it?

Minutes passed, but he couldn't shake the uneasiness caused. Then, a notification popped up on his smart glasses. **ECG malfunction detected.** He froze and mused silently, *"Malfunction?"* He quickly scanned the news feeds, and there it was - reports flooding in about PIXI devices across the city showing faulty readings, especially in their ECG apps. People who had been perfectly healthy were now rushing to hospitals, fearing they were at death's door. Clinics were overwhelmed, emergency lines jammed.

Panic was spreading, all because of a glitch.

Amar felt sweat trickling down his forehead. It wasn't real. He wasn't sick. PIXI had messed up. But the idea had already taken root in his mind. His heart thudded in his chest, harder and faster. What if the glitch was real, but the data was true? Could he trust his own body anymore?

The streets outside were filled with sirens as ambulances raced to deal with the chaos. Social feeds buzzed with panic—people posting about sudden dizziness, irregular heartbeats, a wave of anxiety sweeping over the ultra-connected city. The once-organised machine of the metropolis had turned frantic, all because of a malfunction in the very gadgets that had promised to keep everyone safe.

Amar stood in the middle of his sleek, tech-filled apartment, staring at his PIXI. He ripped it off and threw it onto the bed, but even without it, he could still feel the phantom pulse of the device. Was his heart still beating too fast? Or was it all in his head?

He was part of a system that no longer trusted itself. The pulse of the city, once perfectly timed, had spiralled into chaos. And so had Amar.

As the city outside swelled with panic, Amar stood frozen, unsure of whether to trust the world around him or the one inside his own chest.

Amar's breathing grew shallow as he stared at his PIXI smartwatch lying on the bed, its blank face reflecting the dim light of the apartment. A heavy silence filled the room, broken only by the distant hum of the city's chaos and the soft thrum of his own heartbeat echoing in his ears.

"What if it's true?" he whispered to himself.

He hadn't felt anything wrong before, but now... now every little twinge, every skipped beat felt amplified. His chest felt tight - was it just anxiety, or was something really wrong? He couldn't tell anymore. That's what scared him most. He had become so used to his gadgets telling him how he felt, how he *'SHOULD'* feel that he had lost touch with his own body.

His phone buzzed on the kitchen counter, shattering the eerie quiet. It was a message from Esha, his friend who worked at one of the city's biggest tech firms.

Esha: "Dude, are you okay? PIXI is malfunctioning all over the city! People are losing it! Hospitals are packed. Don't trust it. Just breathe. You're fine."

Amar wanted to believe her, but his hands were already trembling. His phone buzzed again, this time with an alert from - PIXI - *"Critical ECG Failure. Seek immediate medical attention."*

His stomach lurched. Was this part of the malfunction, or was something actually wrong with him? Esha had said not to trust it, but he couldn't stop the dread from creeping deeper into his chest. What if ignoring it meant risking his life?

Another siren wailed outside his window, louder this time. Amar walked over and looked down at the street. Dozens of people were out in the streets, some pacing nervously, others sitting on the kerb, clutching their chests, staring at their smartwatches in disbelief. The city had transformed into a mass of uncertainty - technology, once the pulse of the urban machine, was now the source of panic. He grabbed the watch and wore it again.

Suddenly, his doorbell rang.

He jumped, his heart pounding, and rushed to open it. Esha stood there, out of breath, her eyes wide. She was clutching her own PIXI smartwatch, her face pale with a mix of fear and frustration.

"I had to come," she said, stepping inside without waiting for an invitation. *"It's worse than we thought. The glitch is spreading to other systems too - heart monitors, fitness trackers, even the smart home controls. People are freaking out."*

She grabbed his arm. *"Amar, listen to me. You're fine. We're all fine. It's the tech that's broken, not us. The city's infrastructure is glitching, but people are overreacting because they've forgotten how to trust their bodies."*

Amar nodded, but the tightness in his chest still wouldn't go away.

Esha's eyes softened, sensing his unease. *"We've been living with these things glued to us for so long, we've forgotten how to listen to ourselves. PIXI might be wrong, but we aren't. Come on, let's get out of here - clear our heads."*

Amar hesitated. *"What if it's real? What if I really am—"*

Esha interrupted him, her voice firm but kind. *"Then you'd feel it, wouldn't you? I mean, 'really' feel it. Not because of a screen, but because your body would tell you."*

Amar swallowed hard, but something in her words struck him. He looked down at his wrist, at the PIXI that had ruled his life, and for the first time in years, he felt the urge to just... take it off. To trust his instincts.

He ripped the device from his wrist and threw it onto the kitchen counter next to Esha's.

"There," she said, smiling. *"Now, breathe."*

For a moment, Amar stood still, taking deep breaths, trying to calm the storm inside him. The chaos outside continued, but for the first time all day, he began to feel something other than panic - something like relief.

He could feel his heart, the real one, not the one PIXI measured. And it felt steady, strong, alive.

"Let's get out of here," Esha said, and Amar nodded, grabbing his jacket.

As they stepped out into the chaotic streets, the city buzzed with confusion, screens flashing, people clutching their gadgets like lifelines. But Amar, for the first time in a long while, felt something strange - control. Not from his gadgets or his routines, but from himself.

The city may have fallen into chaos, but Amar was learning to listen to the rhythm of his own heart again.

And that was something no glitch could take away.

As Amar and Esha sat in the park, the peace of the natural world seeping into them, Amar finally felt free from the stranglehold of his devices. The city's distant chaos felt like another world, far removed from the serenity they had found in this tiny slice of nature. For the first time in years, he didn't feel the need to check his vitals, didn't feel the nagging pulse of PIXI telling him how to live.

Hours passed, and the city lights flickered on as the sky deepened into shades of purple and blue. Esha stretched and stood up. *"I should head home, I gotta check on my folks, they're panicking as well,"* she said, smiling. *"You'll be okay?"*

Amar nodded, his heart steady, his mind clearer than ever. *"Yeah, I think I will."*

Esha gave him a wave and walked off, disappearing into the evening crowds. Amar stayed behind for a few more moments, staring up at the sky, enjoying the newfound peace.

But as he finally stood to leave, something strange happened. His phone vibrated in his pocket - a single, urgent buzz. He hesitated for a second, torn between his freedom and the curiosity nagging at him. Reluctantly, he pulled the phone out and glanced at the screen. It was a notification from PIXI, even though he'd removed the watch hours ago.

"Amar, your heart rate has spiked. Possible arrhythmia detected. Seek immediate medical attention."

He frowned. How? He wasn't even wearing the device. He had left it behind in his apartment.

His pulse quickened, and not just from the message. There was no way PIXI could still be monitoring him - was there?

Suddenly, he noticed something else - his smart glasses. He hadn't removed them, and they were still synced to PIXI's cloud. The thought sent a chill down his spine. Could the system still be tracking him even without the watch on his wrist? And if it was, how accurate was it?

Another buzz. ***"Heart rate is increasing. Medical attention advised."***

Amar felt his chest tighten, and not from the message this time. He took a shaky breath, trying to steady himself, but the anxiety was creeping back in. His pulse was rising, and it felt real, not just a figment of his imagination. His mind flashed back to all the people in the streets, clutching their devices, convinced they were dying because PIXI told them so.

He ripped off his smart glasses and stared at them, as if the tiny lenses held all the answers. *Was he really fine?' He was sure of it moments ago, but now? His heart was racing. Was it just panic, or was there really something wrong?*

He had to know.

Abandoning the calm resolve he had found earlier, Amar rushed out of the park, heart pounding, heading for the nearest clinic. The streets were still a frenzy of sirens and people, some rushing towards hospitals, others arguing with each other, their watches buzzing incessantly. Amar barely registered them as he pushed through the crowd, his thoughts a whirlpool of fear and doubt.

By the time he reached the clinic, his heart was pounding out of his chest. He burst through the doors, breathless. The waiting room was packed with people, most of them staring at their devices with wide eyes, panicked breaths, and trembling hands. Amar staggered to the front desk.

"I - I need a check-up. My heart, I think it's... I think it's—"

The receptionist didn't even look up. *"We're full. If you're experiencing symptoms, find somewhere to rest. The tech is malfunctioning. It's all in your head."*

"But what if it's not?" Amar gasped, clutching his chest, genuinely unsure of whether it was panic or something worse. His breath was shallow, his pulse erratic.

"Take a seat," the receptionist murmured, barely paying attention.

Amar collapsed into a chair, staring at the sterile white walls, his heart still pounding. He looked down at his phone. The PIXI notifications were still coming. ***"Critical heart failure detected. Seek medical help immediately."***

His hands trembled as he tried to remember Esha's words, trying to tell himself it was all in his head. But the pounding in his chest felt real. His body felt real. He couldn't shake the feeling that something was wrong.

Then, a voice - faint but distinct - came from his pocket. *"Amar, you need to calm down."*

His blood ran cold. It wasn't a PIXI notification - it was a live voice, someone speaking directly through his phone. He pulled it out, staring at the screen, his heart hammering in his chest.

The screen showed nothing but a blinking light.

"Amar," the voice said again, this time more insistent. *"It's your body. The system is in you now."*

Amar's breath caught. *"What - what are you talking about?"* he stammered, his voice barely above a whisper.

"You didn't think it was just the devices, did you?" The voice was calm, eerily calm. *"The updates, the constant monitoring - it wasn't just data collection. It was an adaptation. The system has learnt you. Integrated with you."*

His phone buzzed again, and Amar's heart leapt as he read the words: ***"Syncing complete."***

His hands shook violently as he looked down at his chest, realising for the first time that the pulsing, the irregular beat he felt - it wasn't just his heart.

It was the system. It was part of him now.

And as the realisation sank in, so did the voice in his ear, cold and certain: *"You can't escape it, Amar. You never could."*

His world spun, the city fading into the background as he collapsed into his chair, his body and mind trapped in a system he could no longer control.

The last thing he saw before darkness took him was the flicker of his smart glasses, back on, showing his vitals - still rising, still syncing, still under control.

But no longer his own.

What does true freedom look like for you, and what steps can you take to achieve it?

THIRTEENTH STITCH

The Love Beyond Biology

By Sneha Singh

Amoha stood there, looking at the rays falling at the forty-five-degree angle. She thought to herself, *"Another evening has arrived and yet again the sun has painted this city with its warm hues of saffron and gold. Yet another evening of looking forward to a desired tomorrow."*

The air in Amoha and Mohnish's house carried the lingering scent of marigolds. They were a typical Marwadi couple in this ancient city of Udaipur, who were completely and very intricately one with the vibrant colours of a joint family. They all lived in their *'pushtaini haveli' (ancestral home)*, and it had sturdy walls made of sandstone and very delicately carved archways. The *'haveli'* stood as living proof to the lives that had unfolded within its walls. Generations whispered through its halls, and laughter lingered on its weathered surfaces.

The corridors had embroidered curtains. Amoha stood behind them, usually, her body language speaking loudly as if she was trying to hide away from the world and anyone's notice. They had a quiet ache that stuck deep-rooted in the hearts of *'Mr & Mrs Mohnish & Amoha Agarwal'*.

Their love story had bloomed amidst the fragrant jasmine vines that climbed the courtyard walls. Mohnish and Amoha had courted for three months after their formal engagement that culminated from an alliance that their parents sought after, for them. Mohnish would often say to Amoha, *"Tumhari aankho mein chupa jadu hai aur yeh mere dil ki sabse khaas baat hai" (In your eyes there lies a hidden magic, and that is the most special thing about my heart).*

His words stirred Amoha's soul, weaving dreams into their shared existence: a mix of hopes, promises, and unspoken desires.

Yet, as seasons turned into years, their union yearned for more. The cradle in the corner of their bedroom remained empty, waiting for the soft weight of a newborn. Amoha would sit by the window, her fingers tracing the embroidered patterns on their curtains, while Mohnish tended to the marigold garden below. The vibrant flowers mirrored their longing, a burst of colour against the backdrop of their silent ache.

One evening, rain-kissed and filled their *'aangan' (courtyard)* with the fragrance of the evening jasmine. Amoha couldn't keep mum any longer, and she broached the subject. She sat on the veranda, her sari billowing like a monsoon cloud, as she watched Mohnish prune the marigolds. The cicadas hummed, and the sky blushed with promise.

"Moh," she began softly, *"do you ever wonder why our home feels incomplete?"*

He looked up, his hands still holding the pruning shears. His eyes etched with laughter and unshed tears. *"Incomplete?"* he mused. *"Perhaps our love story is still unfinished."*

Amoha tilted her head. *"What do you mean?"*

He set the shears aside and joined her on the veranda. *"Our love,"* he said, *"is like these marigolds. Resilient, blooming even in adversity. But it lacks the sweet fragrance of a child's laughter."*

She traced the veins of a marigold leaf. *"We've tried,"* she whispered. *"Months turned into seasons, and seasons into years."*

Mohnish took her hand. *"Our love,"* he said once again, *"is patient. It knows that every chapter has its own timing."*

As raindrops fell, they sat there waiting for the next verse of their love story to unfold. The marigolds danced with the breeze, their golden petals brushing against the embroidered curtains, and so Amoha and Mohnish held onto each other.

And the air held its breath, as if waiting for her next words.

"Moh," she said softly, breaking the silence that had settled between them, *"we should seek help."*

Mohnish, a man of few words, shifted from where he was seated. His eyes flickered with uncertainty. *"What if anyone in the family knows?"* he whispered. *"How will we face them, Moh? We have so many loopholes in our family, the whole samaj (community) will get to know."*

Amoha's resolve hardened. She had carried this ache within her for too long. *"We will face them with courage, until or if they know. We can keep this between each other."* she insisted. *"We deserve more than silent suffering."*

And so, they decided to embark on the journey, the one that led them to Dr Mehta's clinic, tucked away in a quiet corner of Udaipur.

The waiting room at Dr Mehta's smelled of disinfectant and hope. Amoha clutched Mohnish's hand; their intertwined fingers felt like a lifeline to both of them in this unfamiliar territory.

Dr Mehta, a fertility specialist with kind eyes, welcomed them. She spoke of hope to them, *"Let's try the IVF process. It's a bridge between science and miracles." "Hormone injections, tablets, sperm collection, and egg retrieval, it will all feel like a maze but you will navigate through, don't worry,"* she said, assuring them, *"You aren't alone. I have seen countless couples tread this path and their dreams weave into a fabric of possibility."*

As Amoha lay on the examination table, Mohnish stood by her side. The ultrasound machine hummed, revealing secrets hidden within her body. Dr Mehta's voice was gentle as she explained each step: the follicles, the embryos, the fragile chances.

In the quiet of that room, Amoha whispered to Mohnish, *"Our family's story isn't over. It's merely taking a different form."*

He squeezed her hand, his eyes reflecting both fear and determination. *"Together,"* he vowed, *"we'll find our way through this."*

And so, amidst the scent of antiseptic and the echo of whispered prayers, Amoha and Mohnish stepped into the unknown, a couple seeking miracles, while their bond grew stronger than any silence.

They moved through life like tightrope walkers, balancing hope and heartache. Their story, which was once all about the jasmine vines, the romance under the embroidered curtains, and optimism in the moonlight, now bore the weight of an unspoken longing, a childless cradle, and their silent aches.

Amoha's days blurred to and fro from the hospital corridors and waiting rooms. The scent of antiseptic clung to her skin, mingling with the lingering fragrance of marigolds from their courtyard.

Mohnish, always by her side, held her hand during the multiple tests and ultrasounds. His eyes, once filled with laughter, now mirrored her worry. Also, the worry of what would be the effect of so many medicines and hormones that Amoha was swallowing and injecting into herself.

They had furthermore concerns than just this. They had not told the family members what they were going through. Not to the members of their joint family nor to either of their parents. They belonged to a society that would probably more likely just blame Amoha and call her names for not being able to bear a child. Mohnish was very protective of Amoha and vice versa.

Their finances were stretching thin. IVF demanded its toll. They juggled bills, appointments, and whispered conversations in the kitchen. Amoha's bloated abdomen bore the aftermath of hormone injections, each needle pricking a reminder of their shared dream. She counted follicles, tracked her cycles, and prayed for life to take root within her.

The emotional rollercoaster was relentless. Hope surged with each embryo transfer, only to crash when the pregnancy test remained stubbornly negative. Amoha wept in the privacy of their bedroom, her tears absorbed by the embroidered pillow covers. Mohnish was patient and steadfast, holding her close. *"We,"* he murmured, *"are stronger than this struggle, Moh."*

Family gatherings became a masquerade. They laughed, they danced, they celebrated birthdays and weddings. But behind the embroidered curtains of their smiles, pain simmered. Amoha masked her discomfort, the nausea, the fatigue, the fear of another failed cycle. She perfected the art of hiding, even as her body transformed from being hopeful to a battleground of biology.

One evening, after a family puja, Amoha sat on the veranda. The moon hung low, casting shadows on the marigold and jasmine petals. Mohnish joined her, his eyes weary but unwavering. *"How long? We have been through four IVF cycles already, and they have all failed!"* he whispered.

She leaned into his warmth. *"As long as it takes,"* she replied. *"Our family way can't be over just yet, Moh."*

Their hearts held a fragile hope. They whispered prayers into the night, asking for strength, for resilience, for the courage to face each injection leading to yet another disappointment.

On another subsequent day, they were back at the fertility hospital. By this time, all the staff and guards had become part of their journey. They all looked at Mohnish and Amoha with pitiful eyes, as if to say, *"It's okay, this time let's hope it will work out."*

The sterile room was filled with anticipation. Amoha lay on the narrow bed, her fingers tracing the edges of the crisp white sheet. Mohnish stood by her side, his grip on her hand both comforting and desperate. It was another embryo transfer day, their last embryo and hence their last chance.

"Moh," Mohnish whispered, his voice barely audible above the sterile air, *"we've come so far."*

She nodded, her eyes fixed on the ceiling tiles. The tiny vial containing their dreams rested on a tray nearby. It held the promise of life, a fragile hope they dared not shatter.

The doctor entered, her face a mask of professionalism. *"Are you ready?"* she asked, her gloved hands adjusting the equipment.

Amoha closed her eyes. *"Yes,"* she said, her voice steady. *"Let's do this."*

The doctor held Amoha's and Mohnish's hands to form a human chain, and they all prayed together. This was a ritual every time they were transferring an embryo into her.

The procedure was swift, like a combination of science and faith. The embryo, carefully selected, found its new home within her womb. Mohnish watched the ultrasound screen, his heart pounding. *"Hold on..."* he whispered to the tiny cluster of cells. *"Hold on tight."*

Fifteen days later, they sat in their bedroom, the pregnancy test between them. Amoha's hands trembled as she picked it up. The seconds stretched into eternity. Then, the faintest line appeared, showing a whisper of life.

Tears flowed freely, and their secret joy now knew no bounds. Mohnish held her, their hearts overflowing. *"Our miracle,"* he murmured, pressing his lips to her forehead.

They celebrated in the knowledge that there was life growing within Amoha's womb. But they chose silence and made no grand announcements, no celebrations. Just whispered prayers for their unborn child, a fragile soul waiting to be born.

And so, in the quiet of their room, they held onto hope. Mohnish and Amoha looked at each other, *"Our love, our family is weaving into possibility,"* they whispered to each other. *"The waiting room has given way to a new waiting, the countdown to life, Moh!"* Mohnish hushed in the dark.

They whispered promises to the universe, making a silent pact to protect their secret joy until the time was right. Their unborn child, who was now a glimmer of hope, listened from within. Mohnish often spoke to their child, *"Our little cluster of cells, you are a miracle in the making."*

Weeks slipped through their fingers like sand. Each day was like a fragile thread in the fabric of their hope.

The heartbeat tests loomed.

The ultrasound room smelled of Dettol; it felt like a sterile cocoon where dreams and despair collided. Amoha lay there, her heart pounding in sync with the rhythmic hum of the machine. The gel on her abdomen was cool, a stark contrast to the feverish anticipation that gripped her.

Mohnish stood beside her, his calm exterior showing cracks, yet still holding firm. His eyes now carried worry, and his knuckles were white from gripping the edge of the chair.

They had navigated the IVF maze so many times: the injections, the egg retrieval, the embryo transfers, all leading to this moment. The screen flickered, revealing secrets etched in shadows. This time was different. It was their last try and the first time she had tested positive out of all their tries.

The screen flickered to life. It was a portal into their dreams. Their hope hung thicker than any disinfectant in the room. Amoha's eyes were fixed on the monitor, her breath caught in her throat. She had imagined this moment, the flutter of a tiny heartbeat, of their little bundle of joy thriving within her.

But then Dr Mehta's expression shifted, a microsecond of shock. Her eyes widened, her lips parting as if to speak, but the words remained trapped. *"The child, your child, has no heartbeat,"* she spoke, looking sad at the screen.

It shattered their hope, making it all seem like an illusion. Dr. Mehta had delivered news of loss before, but each time was a fresh wound, like a reminder of life's whimsical nature.

Amoha and Mohnish's world had tilted. The room spun, and Amoha clung to the edge of consciousness. Dr. Mehta left them in the room to have a word amongst themselves, in private. *"Dr. Mehta's words are echoing in my ears, Moh, reverberating through my bones. I've felt the flutters, the secret movements within my womb. How could it be gone? How could life slip away so silently?"* Amoha sobbed, holding on to Mohnish.

And then darkness claimed her. Amoha's body crumpled, her limbs started to become heavy. Mohnish caught her, with his own strength, wobbling. His patient facade cracked, and tears spilled down his cheeks. He had been her anchor, her unwavering support, but now he was adrift like a lost sailor in a storm.

"Mohh..!" His voice broke, the syllables raw with pain. He lowered her gently to the floor, his hands trembling. *"Wake up.."* he pleaded. *"Please."*

Dr Mehta's hands moved, checking Amoha's pulse, as she called for assistance. But Mohnish's gaze remained fixed on his wife. Her face was pale, her lips tinged with blue. He brushed her hair back, his fingers tracing the curve of her cheek. *"Come back..."* he whispered. *"I need you."*

And as the medical team rushed in, Mohnish's tears fell freely. He had held their dreams, the cradle, the whispered promises, the future they had painted together. Now it had all slipped away. But in that moment, he vowed, they would find a way to heal. They would carry this grief, this emptiness, and transform it into something meaningful.

Amoha stirred with her eyelids fluttering, whispered faintly, *"Our baby... gone."*

Mohnish cradled her, his heart expanding. *"We'll find hope again,"* he murmured. *"In different forms, different faces."*

Dr Mehta's voice cut through the chaos. *"I'm sorry,"* she said, her eyes mirroring the pain.

But Mohnish knew they would defy despair. They would rise, not as victims, but as survivors. And as he held Amoha, he whispered to their lost child, *"I promise love doesn't need a heartbeat to endure. It needs resilience, open arms, and the courage to face even the darkest days. You go ahead for now little one, until we cross paths again, in a different space, maybe in another time. All the best for your journey ahead."*

In the ultrasound room, where life and loss played their cruel game, Mohnish chose to cling to hope.

The doctor's words hung heavy in the air, a verdict etched in silence. *"I'm sorry again..."* she whispered, with her voice being a fragile bridge between compassion and inevitability.

Their world crumbled. Mohnish's hand trembled as he reached for Amoha's.

Amoha spoke as she sobbed, with broken words, *"We have felt the precipice of creation, with our love a pillar against the darkness. But now, we again stand on the edge of an abyss, staring into the void."* She couldn't speak any further as she kept crying, with tears flowing uncontrollably.

Amoha wept silently, her tears absorbed by the sterile sheets. She had carried life within her. She whispered to Mohnish, *"Why was our little one a fragile spark that flickered out so soon?"* The room blurred, with the ultrasound machine echoing in the distance. She found no meaning in life, in that moment, no solace in the grief they shared.

"Is there anything we could have done differently?" Amoha's voice cracked, the weight of their choices pressing down on both of them.

The doctor shook her head, her eyes kind. *"Sometimes..."* she said, *"Life defies our understanding. It's not your fault."*

But blame was irrelevant. They had loved fiercely, hoped recklessly, and now they mourned, a farewell to a heartbeat that would never echo, leaving footprints of longing in their hearts.

Dr Mehta broke the ice, only for her words to make no sense right at that moment; she was suggesting a thread of possibility. *"Another IVF cycle,"* she said, her voice gentle, *"might be our best chance."*

Amoha's gaze shifted from the sterile room to the window. The sun painted the sky in hues of saffron; this time she didn't see it as something to adore but as something that was mocking her pain. She had trodden this path of the injections, the ultrasounds, the silent prayers just too many times. Each cycle had etched its mark on her soul, leaving scars that no one could see.

Amoha looked at Mohnish and told the doctor, *"We will talk about what we want to do next, Doctor, and then come back to you. Right now, I don't think we can think clearly."* Saying so, the heartbroken duo left the fertility hospital.

Mohnish said, *"Let's not give up. We will come out stronger. It's our duty to keep trying. That's all we have in our hands, Moh."*

But Amoha refused. She couldn't bear another round of hope and then the consequent heartbreak. *"I cannot go through this pain again."* she said, wiping the tears rolling down her cheeks.

Mohnish said, holding Amoha's hand, while still looking straight and holding the steering wheel with others, *"There are other ways to be parents, Moh."*

Amoha's expressions changed, and she kept quiet for a couple of moments, looking out of the window at the passing shops, people, and vendors. Wiping her tears, she said, *"This is what is special about us, Moh. We kept saying our love, our bond is special because we have fallen steep but have risen stronger. This is a eureka moment for me."*

"I see it is for our best to become Yashoda Ma and Nand Baba (Lord Krishna's foster parents). Giving birth is not the only thing that makes a couple parents, but nurturing a child with love and giving the child the best upbringing for sure does!"

Amoha and Mohnish decide to break their silence and sit both of their parents down and tell them all about their IVF journey, their loss, and what brings hope into them again. Their parents wholeheartedly choose the happiness of their children and vowed to support them on this new journey. Both their fathers were friends; they said, *"We feel proud to have raised such children that have grown into such a mature couple at such a young age. Humara aashirwad aur saath hamesha tum dono ke sath hai (our blessing and support will always remain with you both)."* they said.

This conversation changed their line of thought. Months passed in calculating and working things out. They took the path that led to an orphanage amidst the chaos of Udaipur.

There, in the eyes of a little girl named Ananya, they found hope anew.

Ananya, holding the same jasmine flowers in her hands, similar to the ones in Amoha & Mohnish's courtyard, with galaxies and the wonder of a thousand stars in her eyes, clung to Amoha's saree when their eyes first met.

She had lost her parents in a car accident, but her spirit remained unbroken, just like Amoha and Mohnish's.

Amoha watched her twirl and said to Mohnish, *"Did you see how her tiny feet dance across the courtyard's tiles? She is so light in her energy, like she could float."*

Mohnish, smiling with glee in his eyes, replies, *"Yes, and her laughter... it fills the whole haveli, like a sparrow's song. It echoes through every corner, so full of joy."*

"I watch her, twirling and jumping, always so full of life. That sound... her laugh, it is the happiest melody." he said emotionally, still adoring his daughter, looking at her while he spoke to Amoha.

Amoha noticed the joy in Mohnish and with elation in her voice, continued her dialogue with Mohnish, *"It's like our haveli has come alive with her around. Even the quietest corners feel warmer when she giggles."*

The Agarwals stood at the threshold of a new chapter. They had yearned for a heartbeat, a child to call their own. But life had other plans. Ananya became their daughter, the one they would never let go. She brought with her a different kind of love, a love that had them both forget the heartbeat that couldn't thrive.

As they watched her play, Mohnish's strong exterior cracked again, this time with love. His eyes, once etched with grief, softened. *"She's ours,"* he whispered, his voice breaking, *"Our little star."* Amoha nodded, her heart expanding.

Ananya's laughter was a balm, like a reminder that love could bloom even in barren soil. She had filled their home with light, chasing away shadows that had lingered for too long. And so, in the same courtyard where the marigolds once softly shared secrets, the Agarwals accepted their fate.

"Sometimes, love doesn't need a heartbeat, it just needs open arms." Amoha told Mohnish, *"You know when Ananya saw us first, she twirled her small hand gently wrapping around my finger, as if she quietly chose me, in that moment, I just knew, we're a family, stitched together by fate and love, and from that moment on, our hearts were beating as one."*

***

How do you define love in your life? What connections transcend traditional boundaries of love for you?

New beginnings are usually disguised as...

THE END

Get to know the authors through a creative lens!

We are not just best friends; we've also developed into great collaborators on this journey towards our book ***13 Stitches.***

Our writing journey began over 2 years ago, during which we had our fair share of balancing, managing our busy personal lives and professional responsibilities.

Of course! There were days and times when we've both had disagreements, differences of opinions, and frictions, nonetheless, don't we all? Despite the several challenges, our collaboration has come to a strong sense of mutual respect, dedication, and let's just say a mutual feeling of *'comfortable commitment'*. We both brought our best and unique strengths to the table, which has helped our partnership to be more rooted in open communication, trust, and appreciation.

It's what we do best!

We can proudly say that we are tightly woven like a strong fabric that binds us together, rather than tearing us apart.

About the Author

Sneha Singh is a compassionate and dedicated aviator, a corporate communications and marketing professional, also holds a master's in mental health, is very passionate about counselling, and volunteer work with NGOs. She also hosts the podcast Maniya vs Womaniya. Her sentiment for helping others and her love for writing guide her efforts to make a positive impact.

One can follow Sneha on her Instagram page at: **@oldsassysoul**

And you can write to her at iamsnehasingh@gmail.com

Sarab Kaur is a creative spirit - a poet, author, podcaster, homemaker, and devoted mother of two. She has a deep passion for crafting stories and has written two books, Teen Waves and Mini Babbles. Sarab's storytelling extends beyond the written word through her podcasts, Teen Waves Podcasts and Marinated Morals, where her thoughtful insights and narratives connect with listeners around the world.

One can follow Sarab on her Instagram: @**_crispypen_**

And can write to her at sarabsaini316@gmail.com

Did any of our stories resonate with you?

If you found a piece of yourself woven into ***13 Stitches***, we want to hear all about it! Share your thoughts, experiences, or even a favourite moment with us.

Let's connect and celebrate the numerous stories together. Your voice could add a vibrant thread to our narrative!

Through the stitches of our stories, we find connection, understanding, and the beauty of shared journeys.

Connect with us - sarabandsneha@gmail.com

www.ingramcontent.com/pod-product-compliance
Lightning Source LLC
LaVergne TN
LVHW091317150826
845673LV00006B/1674